Gangsters and Ghosts of the Northwoods

By Enid Cleaves

"Gangsters and Ghosts of the Northwoods," by Enid Cleaves. ISBN 978-1-62137-095-6 (softcover).

Library of Congress Control Number on file with publisher.

Published 2012 by Virtualbookworm.com Publishing Inc., P.O. Box 9949, College Station, TX 77842, US. ©2012, Enid Cleaves. All rights reserved. No part of this publication may be reproduced, stored in a retrieval system, or transmitted in any form or by any means, electronic, mechanical, recording or otherwise, without the prior written permission of Enid Cleaves.

Manufactured in the United States of America.

TABLE OF CONTENTS

INTRODUCTION

The Northwoods of Wisconsin and the Upper Peninsula of Michigan are rich in history: logging, mining, railroads, and a vacation destination for the rich and famous...or the infamous, like the mobsters from the greater Chicago area who found solace and secrecy snuggled in the lofty pines and sky blue waters of the remote northern areas.

Gangsters headed north to escape law enforcement officials when things got a little hot. Some started bootlegging businesses here; others, brothels. Possibly, some even buried money or bodies in the secluded forests and lakes. Ghosts of the past still linger in some lodges and inns and, certainly, stories of the colorful past are even more plentiful than the phantoms themselves.

A few residents of northern Wisconsin are still around to remember the likes of gangsters such as John Dillinger, *Baby Face* Nelson and Al *Scarface* Capone. Many more tell stories of their late relatives' relationships with these folk heroes who visited their lodges or employed men in their stills or speakeasies.

Mystery surrounded these gangsters, but it was their generosity, charisma and intrigue that gained them support and respect from the average family who lost their savings when the banks closed, or their jobs when employers could no longer afford to pay them. The liquor business is usually strong when the economy is weak. Needless to say, prohibition was not popular with the families who were facing serious economic problems. Many hired on as bootleggers or operators of moonshine stills. Others just purchased the outlawed beverages.

Ghosts are said to have unfinished business in a place where their spirit roams. Or they may have other reasons for not leaving their old *haunts*. Maybe it's clearing their name, avenging their killers, or searching for something left behind. Some spirits linger where their life was lost; others revisit special places where they may have loved their occupation or perhaps a person who spent time with them there.

Not all the ghosts in the Northwoods are those of gangsters. Yesteryear's lodge owners or residents, maids, waitresses, tribal warriors, family members, and law-abiding citizens from many walks of life roam about in restaurants, homes, lighthouses, and islands. This book is about some shady characters, malevolent ghosts, and dark secrets. But it is also about good ghosts, pranksters perhaps, but nevertheless benevolent.

So, get in the *spirit* to enjoy the following stories!

CHAPTER 1

SCOURGE OF SCARFACE

I can see that sweet Maddona
There's a teardrop in her eye
For her soldier has departed
Left his loved one with a sigh
She said "I will wait forever"
As he sang this last goodbye.
Maddona mia....[1]

Well known mobster Al Capone wrote this love song for his wife from his prison cell in Alcatraz where he was serving time on his 11-year sentence for tax evasion. Mae (Coughlin) Capone *did* wait for him to be released from prison, but life as they knew it would never be the same.

The likes of Al Capone, John Dillinger, Baby Face Nelson and other mobsters frequently traveled from Chicago to the Northwoods of Wisconsin. When law enforcement officials threatened their livelihood and their very freedom, it was time for a little "vacation."

Many Northwoods folks viewed the gangsters as Great Depression folk heroes and were pleased when bank robbers took sizeable withdrawals from the very banks that they blamed for their financial ruin. Plus, winters are long in the north; socializing

---

[1] Verse from "Maddona Mia," Al Capone.

with a few beers or hard liquor was common during those "cabin fever" months—and for that matter the other two or three months too! Men like Capone were not seen as vicious thugs, but well-dressed, generous, and friendly men with exciting lifestyles who made prohibited liquid refreshments available to those who desired them.

Local residents were employed as drivers, "errand boys," and some even operated stills and ran liquor to the Chicago area. Cindy from Minocqua remembers when she was a young girl her dad worked for Capone in a Northwoods still. She recalls having been there once. They had a bell system of some sort to warn the workers to shut down activities if law enforcement agents, or others of suspicion, arrived.

The life of Al Capone

Alphonso Caponi was born January 17, 1899 in Brooklyn, the fourth of Gabriel and Teresa Caponi's nine children. The Caponis were Italian immigrants who had been in the country for about six years. Al was a rebellious and volatile boy who was expelled from school while in the sixth grade after hitting a teacher.

Al felt the school kids looked down on him because of his immigrant working-class status. But he was about to find success in the "land of opportunity" through his criminal activities. He joined the violent James Street gang headed by Johnnie Torrio." In 1918 he went to work as a bouncer in a bar owned by Torrio's friend, Frankie Yale, leader of the Five Points Gang. Capone used his position to justify violent attacks on those he evicted. In one fight Al was cut on his cheek by a knife-yielding opponent, and thus gained the nickname "Scarface." (Later Capone would say he got the scar in World War I; however, he never served a day with the military!)

In early December 1918 Capone fathered a son, Albert Francis (Sonny) with his girlfriend, Mae. They were under 21 years of age, so had to have parental consent to marry—which they did by the end of that month. They moved from Brooklyn to Amityville, Long Island in 1919 to be closer to the rum-running route. The Volstead Act made it "illegal to make, transport, purchase and consume alcohol." There was a large demand for bootlegged liquor, and Capone was eager to capitalize!

Amityville gained notoriety from the book/movie *Amityville Horror* and has had its share of insanity and horror stories to tell. Capone later claimed to be haunted by voices and demons. Maybe they inhabited his body during his stay in the wealthy New York village!? But as far as being an *Amityville Horror* himself while living there, Capone was described as being pretty low key.

Johnnie Torrio moved to Chicago and became leader of the Five Points Gang. In late 1919 he asked Capone join him. Perfect timing: Al was being investigated for killing two men and needed to "get out of Dodge." So he became Torrio's right-hand man, responsible for "loan collecting." Capone was frequently arrested for assault, but never served any time because of Torrio's influence with the authorities.

In May 1920 Torrio brought Capone in on a plot to off his uncle, "Big Jim" Colisimo, brothel owner and leader of a gang bearing his name that ruled Chicago's underground activities. Colisimo had refused to cooperate with Torrio in his efforts to establish speakeasies. So Torrio "offed" Colisimo as well as another rival gang leader: Charles Dion O'Bannion. Gang wars continued for several years after that. In 1924, Capone's younger brother, Salvatore (Frank), was killed while trying to control a mayoral election. He had shot a man in the legs. He then drew his gun on the detectives who dropped him on the spot. Capone ordered that all saloons in Cicero be closed for two hours the night of his brother's burial.

Torrio moved back to Italy in 1925 after an attempt on his life. Capone, now 26, became the Chicago mafia boss. He immediately went about setting up a lucrative bootlegging business in the "windy city," controlling gambling, narcotics, prostitution and protection rackets. He was quite active in bribery, robbery and killings too--quite a job description! At the height of his control, Al allegedly had numerous city and state officials, as well as half of the Chicago police force, on his payroll!

From the day he arrived in Chicago as a rough-and-tumble, crude-but-calculating gangster with little polish, Capone learned well from his mentor Torrio. He developed smooth and suave social graces necessary for projecting an image compatible to a well-heeled politician, philanthropist and family man. He opened soup kitchens to feed the poor and bought clothing for needy families. He supplied materials and services (albeit illegal) to the general public that they desired and even demanded.

Several attempts were made on Capone's life, but with a lot of luck and several trusted bodyguards (one of them being Frank Gallucio—the man responsible for the *Scarface* nickname) he managed to escape harm.

Two of his bodyguards planned an assassination attempt on Capone. When he became aware of this, he planned a banquet in their honor. At the event, he presented a toast. The story diverges here: The popular version has Capone suddenly grabbing a club and brutally beating both men to death. The other is that Tony Accardo, acting under Capone, did the dastardly deed. Accounts say Accardo suddenly took on the nickname *Joe Batters*. Perhaps the real version is contained in Deirdre Capone's book: *Uncle Al Capone, The Untold Story From Inside His Family.* Capone, granddaughter of Al's brother, Ralph, describes a conversation with her grandfather:

> I know of one time my grandfather called the Baseball Incident. There were two guys that worked for Al who went behind the scenes and tried to get the chef to poison his food because someone put a $500,000 bounty on his head.
>
> When Al found out, he turned to my granddad and said, 'I think we should have a little party,' when they attended they didn't leave....

The author then goes on to say that the unfortunate victims were beaten to death with baseball bats by Al and Ralph Capone and some of their associates.

And it is well known that Capone often had subordinates do his dirty work. Take the St. Valentine's Day Massacre in 1929. Seven members of *Bugsy* Moran's gang were gunned down while meeting in a Chicago garage. Dressed as policemen,

Capone's henchmen ordered the men to stand against the wall. Believing it was just a routine shakedown, they turned around and put their hands on the brick wall. Then they were gunned down with sawed-off shotguns and submachine guns. The real target was Moran himself, but it turns out Moran was late for his own meeting. (Some say he thus probably delayed his eternal meeting with Satan.) Details on the massacre vary too, but it is generally thought that Al Capone himself was not present. No one was ever charged for the vicious crime.

Capone made money transfers under fake or borrowed names. He had virtually no assets in his own name. (The title of his Chicago home was under his mother's and sister's name, and his wife's name was on the title of the Florida mansion.) Capone paid off many men who had some incriminating evidence on him.

"Get Capone!"

President Herbert Hoover decided to fight Capone on two fronts: income tax invasion and prohibition violations. Elliot Ness headed up the latter. Ness depended upon an extensive wire-tapping operation to yield information that led to raids on breweries and stills. Several operations were closed down. Capone responded with bribery offers, and even assassination attempts, but Ness remained undaunted. Ness and his agents became known as "The Untouchables."

In the end it was one IRS agent, Frank Wilson, who brought Capone to justice. Though Capone reported no income, the IRS estimated over $1 million in expenses during the period 1924-29. They felt he must have an income if he had that amount (and more) of expenses! Capone claimed later that he did not know he had to pay taxes on income from illegal activities! Wilson also was able to come up with some receipts that linked Capone to illegal gambling. He infiltrated one of his agents, Michael Malone, into the gang. Malone played cards with the boys at the Lexington Hotel. They slowly came to accept the Italian-looking Malone as one of their own. He passed himself off as a wanted gangster from Philadelphia. (Malone worked undercover at Ralph Capone's hotel in Mercer, Wisconsin. He appeared as a witness in 1951 in the tax case against Ralph.)

Another informant was Edward O'Hare, co-owner of a lucrative dog track with Capone. O'Hare was a legal advisor/business manager to Capone as well. O'Hare provided information to the IRS in exchange for his son getting into (and staying at) the Naval Academy at Annapolis. Other accounts say it was done to keep himself out of prison. So maybe it was a bit of each. As a result, Capone was convicted of several tax evasion counts and sentenced to eleven years in a federal penitentiary. At that point, Capone physically assaulted the jury foreman and was taken away to his cell. On November 8, 1939, a man yielding a shotgun pulled up next to O'Hare's car and fired two fatal shots into his neck and head. Eddie was the father of Butch O'Hare, renowned World War II fighter pilot whose name graces Chicago's international airport.

After several months of appeals on his tax evasion charges, Capone was transferred to Atlanta State Penitentiary, and two years later was transferred to Alcatraz Island off San Francisco. Here Capone formed a prison "band." He played a banjo that his wife had given him. Until recently, it was not known that he had written a song for her entitled *Maddona Mia* Apparently, someone was a poor speller (see picture below), but *madonna mia* translates to English as "my lady." ABC News ran a special in April 2009 on Capone's jailhouse music, describing the composition as a "killer's love song for his wife."

Capone's only known original song

Capone was released from prison on November 19, 1939. He had lost weight and had signs of severe dementia, probably caused by a long-standing bout with syphilis. In fact, he spent the last year of his sentence in a mental institution. He retired quietly to his Florida mansion and passed away there on January 25, 1947.

Capone's siblings

Raffael Capone, a few years younger than his brother Al, became known as Ralph when he joined his brother in the U.S. in 1922. Nicknamed *Bottles*, Ralph was the director of liquor sales for the mob. He sold mineral water and ginger ale for the

Waukesha Waters Company to restaurants (for mix) and illegal beer to various speakeasies. He also was a cigarette vendor and ran a bookmaking operation. During the height of his career, he was the mob's cashier. At that time the mob was allegedly making about $6 million per week!

Ralph was convicted for tax invasion. He finally did file a return, but for only a fraction of what he really made. Feds found a previously unknown bank account that sealed the case. Ralph was sentenced to prison in November 1931 and was released for good behavior on February 27, 1934.

In the early 1940s Ralph and his wife purchased the Rex Hotel (previously known as Billy's Bar) in Mercer, Wisconsin. Ralph also owned the Recap Lodge at Martha Lake and reportedly shared ownership of Beaver Lodge with "Greasy Thumb" Guzik, another Chicago gambling syndicate head. While Al Capone was in prison, the two men supposedly ran the mob.

Ralph lived out his life in Mercer, Wisconsin. My aunt and uncle, Marguerite and John, lived there in the early 70s. They met Ralph at the local Senior Center and echoed many sentiments that Ralph was very well liked, friendly and generous.

Peg Brunner of the Mercer Area Historical Center remembers her dad's stories of Ralph driving into downtown Mercer every Christmas in a horse-drawn hay wagon. He gave out packages filled with oranges, apples, candy, etc. to every kid there. Peg also relates that Ralph was in town one cold day in the late autumn or early winter and saw a boy lightly dressed in tennis shoes and a windbreaker. He bought the kid some boots, socks and a winter jacket at the local Wampum Shop. When the kid went home, his parents accused him of stealing the items. They eventually called the shop, and the clerk confirmed that it was Ralph who made the purchase! Ralph Capone died in November 1974 at a nursing home in nearby Hurley after being ill for many years.

Peggy Brunner, Mercer Area Historical Society, enjoys talking about the gangster heydays.

Salvatore (Frank) Capone tried to control the Cicero 1924 mayoral elections by kidnapping and even shooting supporters of his opponents. Frank was killed outside of the polling station when he drew his gun on detectives. His cousin also died in that gunfight.

The "Lost Capone" brother, Vincenzo, changed his name to Richard Hart after serving in the U.S. Army during World War I. That name was taken from a famous cowboy. Richard, also known as *Two-Gun,* established a career in law enforcement! Umberto was an employee of the Cicero Tribune, owned by Al. He changed his last name to Raiola in 1942. Erminio, called John or Mimi, changed his name to Martin. He served prison terms for minor offenses like vagrancy. Amedeo, called Matthew, was a tavern owner.

There were two sisters too. Rose was born and died in 1910. Mafalda, born in 1912, married John Maritote. Though she was not directly involved in racketeering, her brother-in-law, Frank Maritote, was a mob affiliate jailed for extortion in 1943.

The Hideout

A quaint old building sits on a beautiful 400-acre setting about six miles north of Couderay, Wisconsin. It is the *Hideout*; Capone purchased this fortress in 1925, when he was 27 years old.

As you drive into the estate off Highway CC (about 17 miles southeast of Hayward) you notice the stone guard tower where men stood watch over the hideout when Capone was present. Two German shepherd dogs paroled the perimeter of the property throughout the night. Trees grow in and around the tower today. There are more trees today due to heavy logging early last century.

My husband and I signed up for the tour and met our guide outside. He showed us through the 18-inch-thick fieldstone-walled home. We looked around as we listened to the audio portion of the tour. It was easy to imagine yourself as that fly on the wall watching Capone and his mobster friends play a high-stakes poker game in front of the massive stone fireplace:

Two bottles of bootlegged whisky adorn the card table; the men take turns pouring it into heavy glasses. A couple of women wearing flapper-style dresses with matching shoes sit at the dining table, smoking cigarettes. They are not allowed at the high-stakes card game in the adjoining room!

The dogs began to bark. Capone rushes up one of the custom-made spiral staircases to the upstairs bedrooms and turns on the floodlights. It is just the seaplane coming in from Canada. Liquor is legal there. Tonight is the night for the delivery; tarpaulin-covered trucks are waiting at the dock to load the hard liquor. In a day or two the booze will be sold in the speakeasies of Chicago.

Living quarters at the Hideout near Couderay, WI

37-acre Cranberry Lake nestled within the Hideaway estate

There is a small dugout prison on the property. A home-made cement mixer sits outside the cell! You get the picture! The bottom of the lake supposedly is composed of "sinking mud." I noticed a skull on the ground behind the bars and asked our guide, "I assume that skull in there is a prop??" He replied in a feigned seriousness, "There's a skull in there?"

The old 8-car garage has been converted into a nostalgic restaurant, a gift shop and an ice-cream parlor. There is a caretaker's cottage, a bunkhouse and maintenance shed. A barn once held chickens that provided Capone with fresh eggs for breakfast, and a garden once produced fresh vegetables.

Tours are given during the summer months. Displays include memorabilia of Elliot Ness and the Untouchables and the St. Valentine's Day Massacre. An audio account of that day brings you up to the final moment—the gunfire. Then the curtain is pulled open, and you view the bloody massacre scene!

Promotional brochure

Capone loved to fish the Turtle Flambeau Flowage, especially in the years after he was released from prison. The flowage is near Mercer where brother Ralph retired. In his latter days "Big Al" revisited there, perhaps a quieter, more reflective escape in his dementia-deteriorated brain than in his horrible heyday past.

The property was purchased by Guy and Jean Houston in 1959 for a reputed $4.25 million. It was sold to the Chippewa Valley Bank of Wisconsin for $2.6 million in October 2009. Supposedly, they were the only bidders because nobody was allowed onto the property prior to its sale. The nostalgic value is priceless! In the spring of 2010 after bankruptcy hearings, the Hideout was purchased from the bank by the Lac Courte Oreilles Tribe.

There are many ghost stories connected with Al Capone. His apparition was spotted by a worker doing some remodeling on the fourth floor at the Elm Hotel in Excelsior Springs, Missouri. Another worker saw a ghost of a man wearing a Panama hat on the second floor. Still others felt an "eerie presence" was watching them in a third-floor room.

Many reports come from Allegan County in lower Michigan. Reports tell of a yellow glow around the ruins of a resort. People claim to have been chased by ghostly white dogs there. And Capone's ghost car has been seen on the county's back roads. Supposedly, Capone held secret meetings in underground tunnels in the area and buried some bodies in the quicksand near the site of the resort. Members of the area's Historical Society have confirmed that remains of what seems to be the resort and the tunnels do exist. They also confirmed that one of the participants in the St. Valentine's Day Massacre hid weapons in his home in Berrien County that were used in the slaying. Historical records state that the Capone gang hung out in Benton Harbor's "Little Italy" section and in St. Joseph, specifically at the Whitcomb Hotel, but they haven't been able to verify the ghosts!

Owners of the 75-year-old Hide-A-Way Resort and Restaurant in Hazlehurst, Wisconsin (not to be confused with the Hideout) reside in their living quarters beneath what were former brothel rooms here. At night they sometimes hear sounds of "high heels walking on the wooden floor upstairs." Stories tell of "Capone's goons guarding the driveway with Tommy guns."

After Capone died in 1947, prison guards at Alcatraz reported hearing banjo music coming from his old cell. While Capone was an inmate here, he complained that the spirit of James Clark, a victim of the St. Valentine's Day massacre, haunted him continually. In fact, that demon had been with Capone since about 1929, shortly after Clark's death. He even contacted a psychic in 1931, but obviously she was not able to rid him of the evil spirit that haunted him until his dying days.

Al Capone is buried in Mt. Carmel Cemetery on the west side of Hillside, Illinois. A stone monument partially covered by plant growth stands over a flat marker bearing his name and the dates 1899 – 1947. "My Jesus, Mercy" is engraved at the bottom of the marker. Cemetery custodians often find cigars, flowers, coins, or a bottle of alcohol that has been placed on top of the marker.

Maybe it is because the ghost of James Clark followed Capone to his grave that Big Al's spirit is not here. No unusual activities have been noted at the cemetery. Capone's spirit may move around from Missouri to Michigan to his old prison cell at Alcatraz. There he can be left alone in his cell, in peace, to play his beloved banjo!

CHAPTER 2

GENTLEMAN JOHNNY

I much admire, I must admit
The man who robs a Bank.
It takes a lot of guts and grit,
For lack of which I thank the gods...

I think he is the kind of stuff
To be a mighty man
In battlefield,--aye, brave enough
The Cross Victorian
To win and rise to high command,
A hero in the land.

What General with all his swank
Has guts enough to rob a Bank!.[2]

I wrote of John Dillinger in one of my previous books, *Ghostly Tales of Lake Michigan.* I told of his path of bank robberies and shootings that led to jail terms, escapes, and bold escapades.

In January 1934 Dillinger was jailed at Crown Point, Indiana for a bank heist in which a policeman was killed. A little over a month later he broke out of jail with a fake wooden gun that he whittled using a washboard and painted black with shoe polish! To add insult to injury of having

---

[2] Verse from "Bank Robber," Robert W. Service.

broken out of an "escape proof" jail, Dillinger stole the female sheriff's brand-new V-8 Ford!

In early March Dillinger had joined up with other gang members (who were not serving time) and robbed a bank in Sioux Falls, South Dakota. Dillinger received a shoulder wound in a shootout as the gang escaped with bank-customer hostages standing on their running boards as shields. A doctor in St. Paul attended his wound, and Dillinger laid low for a short time in a rented apartment he shared with his girlfriend, Evelyn (Billie) Freschette. It wasn't long before the landlord figured out who his tenants were and called the police. In another exchange of gunfire, Dillinger escaped out of the back door of the apartment. Billie was arrested for harboring a criminal and sentenced to two years in a St. Paul jail.

Dillinger returned to Indiana and on April 13 stole guns and three bulletproof vests from the Warsaw, Indiana police station. They retreated to Sault Ste. Marie, Michigan to stay with a gang-member's sister there.

On April 20, Dillinger, along with gang members John Hamilton, Baby-Face Nelson, Homer Van Meter, Tommy Carroll, their wives and girlfriends, as well as a friend of the gang, Pat Reilly, arrived at Little Bohemia, a lodge on Little Star Lake in Manitowish Waters, Wisconsin. It was here that the feds staged a surprise attack that led to innocent people being killed. On the infamous day—April 22, 1934—as shots were allegedly exchanged at Little Bohemia, Dillinger escaped down a bank behind the lodge, ran unnoticed along Little Star Lake, stole a car, and headed for St. Paul.

Darlene Beach recalled the night of April 22 very well. She was on her way to have dinner at Little Bohemia that evening when "something told me that we must not go in there, and I refused to go. We stopped by the side of the road and argued about it; they were all mad at me." It was at that moment that "a car roared past us, throwing gravel all over. Later we figured it was one of Dillinger's friends." The small group went instead to a restaurant in downtown Manitowish Waters to find the door locked. The owner recognized the party and let them in. He "was a deputy sheriff and said he had received a call that Dillinger was at Little Bohemia." The car Beach was riding in was "right behind John Hoffman and his two companions" who DID go into Little Bohemia for a couple of beers and were shot mistakenly by FBI. Hoffman was seriously injured; one of the other men was killed.

(Note: Darlene Sell-Beach, along with Vergie Flesch and Peggy Brunner, founded The Mercer Area Historical Society. Brunner and Beach were contributing authors to "Mercer Remembers...Pictures & Stories of its Past.")

Peggy Brunner's dad claimed the escape report was incorrect; that Dillinger really escaped in a boat moored at the dock and no shots were exchanged, except for those fired by the FBI agents. Brunner's dad worked for the Conservation Department (now the DNR) and says that (being hunters and excellent shots) they were asked to go to the bridge by Koerner's Resort (where the Blue Bayou sits today) and intercept the gangsters. But, because they were civilians and had families, it would be too dangerous.

Bullet holes remain in the windows at Little Bohemia. There is a display of paraphernalia left behind: a shaving kit, ammunition, a vintage hat, a ladies high-heeled shoe, and even a seat from the Biograph Theatre where Dillinger was attending a movie the night he was killed! Brunner's dad offered the idea that the bullet holes in the windows were put there the day after the raid by owner Emil Wanatka. Others say Emil just enhanced the scene!

The local paper (1937) reported that Dillinger's father (also named John) came to the Northwoods to "be in charge of the museum at Little Bohemia where the personal belongings of the late John Dillinger and members of his gang are kept." It said that the 73-year-old man was "accompanied by his daughter, Miss Frances, 15 years of age."

With certainty, it was here at Little Bohemia that Johnnie Depp, Christian Bale and other Hollywood actors came in April 2008 to "shoot" the famous shootout. The movie, *Public Enemies*, was released in July 2009.

Promotional poster features
actor Johnny Depp

I talked with an extra in the movie, Jerry Wagner, a local self-employed caretaker and maintenance man. Jerry provided an insight into how he got the job and just what went on at the closed movie set at the end of the long drive off Highway 51. Jerry's comments are paraphrased below.

> My girlfriend, Jeanne, saw a notice on the bulletin board at the Soda Grill looking for extras. I sent in my picture on a Wednesday and got a phone call the following Monday from the casting agency out of Chicago.
>
> I went to Oshkosh where I filled out a basic information sheet and received vouchers for pay ($65 day plus overtime after 8 hours). I had a beard and long hair; they cut that off immediately.
>
> We arrived for work about 6 p.m. each day. The costume designer looked us over on a daily basis to make sure that we looked exactly like we did when we left the day before. We shot on an average about one or two hours a day. The rest of the time we spent waiting at the base camp (the Catholic church down the highway about a mile) or inside a cabin at Little Bo.
>
> We ate very well: Lobster, steak, etc., usually about 1-2 a.m. We had lunch earlier in the evening, and there were always sandwiches and snacks available from any of three tents on the premises.
>
> They told us not to ask anyone for autographs or talk to the actors unless they spoke to us first. Most of them were pretty

nice. There was this English actor, Stephen Graham, who played Baby Face Nelson. He came in talking in a Brooklyn accent. Johnny Depp replied in his pirate tone (from his well-known *Pirates of the Caribbean* movies), and it was a lot of fun listening to their exchange.

The shootout scene was interesting. I was the bartender. A young couple is having dinner at a table. Baby Face is leaning on the bar with a machine gun under his arm pit. Everyone is scared because he is drunk. He is asking people to stay, but finally allows the CCC men to leave as they said they had to get up early next morning for work.

(Note: The CCC men were the locals who were mistaken for gang members as the Wanatka's dogs began to bark when the men left the restaurant. They did not hear the Feds shout "Halt" due to the barking dogs and their blaring car radio)

Nelson buys a drink for the couple having dinner and says to the man, "Is this your wife, you stupid egg?"

Shortly thereafter, gunshots are heard outside. We hit the floor! Nelson starts knocking out the windows and shooting. Dillinger is upstairs and leaves out a back window, jumping off the roof.

Three cameras provide a broad view of the shooting. Men shoot clear plastic balls out of paintball guns, unseen by the cameras. All of the bottles of liquor were replaced with sugar glass—as were the windows in the room. As the scene evolved, we hit the floor! The breakaway glass exploded everywhere. The plates of food 'blew up' and one of the extras taking cover under the dinner table was covered with his pork chop dinner for the rest of the scene!

Jerry went on to say that it was interesting and awesome to appear in the film and see it being shot. He formed close friendships during the long hours they spent waiting to be called. As we spoke, he was planning a reunion party with other area extras to relive their once-in-a-lifetime experience!

Jerry Wagner, with hair grown back,
appears at local movie premier

Movie premier reception at Little Bohemia in July 2009

In July 2011 an event organized by researcher/ author Larry Schroeder from Wausau, Wisconsin was held at Little Bohemia. The grand nephew of John Dillinger, Jeff Scalf; family and friends of Dillinger's girlfriend, Evelyn "Billie" Freschette; as well as extras who appeared in *Public Enemies* were in attendance. Diedre Capone, granddaughter of Ralph Capone, was expected to sign copies of her book, "Uncle Al—the Untold Story from Inside His Family." She was driving to Manitowish Waters and supposed turned back somewhere in central Wisconsin because of inclement weather.

Jeffery Scalf, grand nephew of John Dillinger.

Scalf provided an interesting talk about John Dillinger, brother of his grandmother, Doris. He corrected all of us who have pronounced "Dillinger" like *Ginger*. The name is pronounced like *Grr* as a dog would growl: *Dillin Grr*. Scalf says "the family does not romanticize or vilify John" and adds that "He wasn't vicious or a killer, but what he did was wrong." Today Scalf heads up the John Dillinger Troubled Youth Fund. All profits from fundraisers and sales will go to help to steer young people away from crime as well as aid those who have been victimized by crime.

Scalf went on to say that, even though Dillinger was charged with killing Chief of Police Patrick O'Malley during the West Chicago bank robbery, it was really gangster John Paul Chase who did the deed. Witnesses at the scene knew there was a *John* present, but only assumed it was Dillinger. (He was actually in Florida at the time.)

The *Jackrabbit* nickname that we have heard to describe Dillinger's ability to vault (no pun intended) over bank counters and such, just isn't true. A popular nickname was *Gentleman Johnny*, a term describing his practice of taking money from banks, but none from the customers. John was a charismatic and congenial guy with a knack for keeping the gang together as "a cohesive unit."

Town resident Ruth Gardner, provided period furniture and antiques to be used in the upstairs sleeping rooms for the film. The items came from Voss's Lodge on Highway 51. Ruth owns and runs the family resort. Her mother, Audrey, was a sister to Emil Wanatka Sr.'s wife Nan. Audrey lived with the Wanatkas for a time. The following are excerpts from Ruth's interview in 2008 with a reporter for the *Rhinelander Daily News*:

> Emil wanted Dillinger and his gang to leave just before the shootout. My Aunt Nan had slipped a note into my grandmother's cigarette pack telling them who the visitors were. They went to Rhinelander and called the FBI. Emil and Nan were hiding in the walk-in freezer when the shootout was going on....
>
> There was always a rumor of a stash of money left by Dillinger at Little Bohemia. Nobody ever found the money, but Emil lived awfully well for a resort owner.

Wanatka's son discredits the story that the gang left behind a reported $200,000 as they fled the Northwoods. If anyone ever found loot belonging to the gang, it continues to be a very well kept secret. Jeff Scalf stated pretty emphatically, "There is no buried money."

Only three months after the Manitowish Waters shootout, Dillinger was shot and killed outside the Biograph Theatre in Chicago. He was betrayed by the "Lady in Red," Anna Sage, a madam who made a deal with authorities in hopes of avoiding deportation. (That did not happen; Sage was eventually returned to Romania.) Sage, John and his latest girlfriend, Polly Hamilton, attended the movies that evening. Anna dressed in a red-orange colored skirt to be recognized by the federal agents.

Some believe that the man gunned down outside the Biograph was not John Dillinger but a look-alike hood named Jimmy Lawrence who had moved to the area from Wisconsin. Many believe that Polly Hamilton thought she was dating Lawrence. Whether she still believed that after her landlord, Anna, discovered the real truth is questionable. Possibly, she was even in on the ambush.

There seemed to be discrepancies in the autopsy and the facts. Even John's father reportedly said upon viewing the body, "That's not my son." Some say letters were received from Dillinger postmarked from the West Coast after his alleged death. Lawrence seemed to disappear after that night too.

A ghostly figure is sometimes seen running into the alleyway next to the theatre. Whether it is Dillinger, or possibly Lawrence, one might only *specter-rate.* Some scenes from "Public Enemies" were shot in Chicago. Maybe John was looking down, pleased that a movie was being made of his life and totally enjoying the notorious, yet benevolent, reputation that he carried with him throughout his shortened adulthood.

There are many connections to Dillinger that still surface today. Persons from the next generation following those men involved in the April 1934 shootout still live here. Stories abound—and they can be as different as those telling the stories. But all of the versions are interesting to say the least.

Peggy Brunner used to live near Brunner Road and Highway H in Mercer. At the time there was a landing field there. She reminisces:

> The children were warned to stay away from any plane that came in. We used to watch the planes come in. One day a plane landed, and a limo came to pick up the occupants. Another limo came to pick up people to go to Winegar. That limo was used to pick up FBI men who were tailing the first limo.
>
> I was with my dad that evening and we went up to see. We saw some tires along the road, and I asked "What are those tires doing there?"
>
> 'Oh, Dillinger was here; the FBI men were chasing them. He shot the tires off their car.'

Peggy went on to say that Dillinger was a frequent visitor to Wisconsin's Northwoods, staying at a variety of places, including Little Bohemia. On this particular trip he was apparently headed a little further north.

I found that I have a few distant connections to John Dillinger:

Our son-in-law's mother claims Dillinger married her cousin. A fellow from my hometown married the daughter of Robert Johnson, the man kidnapped by Dillinger in his own vehicle.

Years ago, my next-door neighbor met a man named Walter Conroy who was in the Northwoods to do some deer hunting. Larry became friends with this police chief from Gary, Indiana who claimed to be "closest to Dillinger" when he was shot and killed outside the Biograph Theatre. Conroy told Larry that he should get a snowmobile for his kids. Larry replied, "I can't afford to do that." Then, every week, a $100 bill came in the mail until there was enough to buy a snowmobile!

(Note: That story seems be substantiated by an article in a reproduction newspaper, "Historical FishWrap," that states four police officers from Chicago and Indiana were involved in the stakeout at the Biograph that night. They were told they could receive the reward money if Dillinger was captured. Federal agents were not allowed to accept rewards—but they would receive the glory!

Arthur Brunner, another local man and friend of Larry's, told a similar story. Art's father was a close family friend of the Conroys. The story, passed down to Brunner, later to Larry and now to me, is that Walter Conroy was standing over Dillinger and finished him off with three bullet holes to the chest.

Jeff Scalf told me Dillinger had only $7 and some odd change in his pocket when he died. But his money belt, usually containing about $10,000, was missing. "John's dad tried to get him to give up the criminal lifestyle," to which John replied, "I can't; I've gone too far." But, Scalf said that John planned to retire in South America after just one more job: a train robbery. That train left the station!

29

There are as many varieties in the stories told as there are fish in the sea. Many are just fish tales, but each of us can cast aside the ones we don't accept, and reach our own net conclusions!

But one thing that we can believe, like Robert Service says in his poem at the beginning of this chapter, is that John Dillinger had what it takes to rise to a position of high command: charisma, leadership abilities, strength and agility—all of this and "guts enough to rob a bank!"

CHAPTER 3

BABY FACE

**Born Lester Joseph Gillis
An ill tempered brat
He terrorized the neighborhood
With a wooden baseball bat[3]**

Lester Gillis was born on December 6, 1908 in Chicago to Belgian immigrant parents, Josef and Mary Gillis. It was a difficult change from the quiet beautiful countryside in Cape Breton, Nova Scotia where Josef worked in the stockyards and Mary tutored school kids in French.

The adolescent Lester, called George by his parents, readily took to the "hood." He was small in stature and often picked on by the neighborhood tough guys. Armed with a switchblade, he soon became a vicious fighter. Gillis was a successful car thief by his early teens. He chummed with the likes of Roger *Terrible* Touhy and other future notorious gang members who gave him the nickname *Baby Face* because he looked younger than his years, even at that time. (Touhy, like so many other Chicago gangsters, loved to escape to Wisconsin's Northwoods. He visited places like Ma Bailey's bordello—later a supper club—in Minocqua.)

---

[3] Verse from "Baby Face Nelson," Day Torrey.

At age 14 Gillis was sentenced to a boys' home for auto theft. While he was incarcerated, his father committed suicide. One of the reasons given was Josef's chagrin over his son's criminal activities. Gillis internalized that fact and began to support his mother and siblings with the money he stole.

Released on parole in two years, Gillis was arrested for robbery again within five months. Reportedly, the judge was not happy when Gillis told him where he could go, and sent him to the Chicago Boys Home. Here he would be stay for several months, until the end of 1926.

It wasn't long after his release that Gillis was heading up a protection racket back in his old neighborhood. His ruthless reputation led to his next job as an enforcer for Al Capone. About this time Gillis informally changed his name to George Nelson.

In the post-Volstead-Act era of Capone-controlled Chicago, one of Capone's top men, Jack McGurn, was told to hire a group of *enforcers*. Word spread, Nelson submitted his resume, and soon joined the group. After a period of time, though, Capone began to feel that Nelson was too much of a hothead and blood-letter—even for him. McGurn fired him, and Nelson returned to an occupation he knew well: armed robbery.

Nelson had just turned 22 when he presented an engagement ring (paid for by a recent jewelry store heist) to a 16-year-old sales clerk at a Woolworth's store named Helen Wawrzyniak. They married, had a family and remained together for the rest of *his* life. Helen would receive the Gillis name, though Gillis himself was pretty much known to others now as Baby Face Nelson. He hated the nickname, but it became so widely used that he could not fight it. Besides, he had bigger fights to win. The next one would be escaping incarceration.

Nelson was arrested for another jewelry store hit in early 1931 and sent to Joliet Penitentiary. While there, he was also charged with a robbery in Wheaton, Illinois that stood to add another 25 years onto his current sentence. In February 1932, Nelson was being transported to a hearing when he insisted that he was nauseated and needed to use the restroom. The guard foolishly removed the handcuffs, at which time Nelson accosted him, jumped off the train, and jumped into a waiting getaway car driven by his wife.

They headed for California; specifically, Sausalito— home to Sicilian mob boss Joe Parente. It was in Sausalito that Nelson would be introduced to Tommy Carroll, Eddie Green, (associates of John Dillinger) and John Paul Chase. Chase was involved with smuggling Parente's liquor, and would become Nelson's lifelong friend.

In May 1933 Nelson headed for Long Beach, Indiana. Here he would meet several criminals. The most noted was Homer Van Meter, who had connections with the John Dillinger gang. And, coincidentally, Nelson would run into Carroll and Green who were now in Indiana. Chase joined Nelson in December 1933. The two traveled to Reno, Nevada.

Nevada historian, writer and publisher Rich Moreno relates a story about a man named Roy Frisch. Frisch was a cashier at the Riverside Bank who had ties with a couple of Reno gamblers involved in a wire-fraud scheme. One of the men owned the Riverside bank and allegedly was laundering money through his bank. Fritch was to be the government's main witness against the two men at an arraignment scheduled for April 2, 1934. On March 22, Fritch walked to a movie. After the movie, he was spotted returning to his home. He never arrived. Moreno states that according to FBI files, Nelson and Chase were in Reno during that time period. Chase supposedly later told the FBI that Nelson had killed a man who was to testify in a fraud case, and that he dumped the body in an abandoned Nevada mine shaft.

Next, Chase and Nelson would pair with Carroll and Green for a series of bank robberies throughout Nebraska, Iowa and Wisconsin. Nelson was the self-appointed leader of the group and the most vocal and vicious. Bank employees who did not go with the program would be spattered with bullets from Nelson's submachine gun.

Sometimes Helen would come along. She stayed in the backseat of the car, but loved the excitement and delighted at the dashing, demanding, daunting demeanor of her husband.

Then, in early 1934, Nelson and Chase joined up with the Dillinger gang, giving them a new-found notoriety. Dillinger was now No. 1 on J. Edgar Hoover's Public Enemy list. (When Dillinger was killed later that year, Nelson took over the title—one that he had long coveted.)

In April of 1934 Nelson accompanied several of the Dillinger gang to northern Wisconsin. Chase did not come with them. They headed to Emil Wanatka's Little Bohemia in Manitowish Waters.

You know the scenario: FBI agents arrived at Little Bohemia the night of April 22, 1934, dogs began to bark. At that time three men came outside, got into their auto, and headed down the long driveway to the highway. The G-men shouted "Halt," but they were not heard and shots were fired at the car. One man was killed and the other two injured. They were not gang members but locals who had just left the bar. Dillinger's gang was alerted and fired back from within the lodge.

Nelson and his wife were staying in a cabin near the main lodge. He grabbed his weapon and fired into the night. The gang was outnumbered, and they fled down the embankment behind the lodge and along the lake. Nelson was the only one who headed south.

After stumbling through the brush and snow for maybe 40 minutes, Nelson came upon a resort where he took the owners, Mr. and Mrs. Lang, as hostage in their own auto. Heading south on the highway he saw lights at a house. He turned off the car lights and continued to the driveway of the home. It was Koerner's Resort.

Emil Wanatka and his two bartenders were picked up on the highway by Emil's brother in law. They headed for the Koerners, too, presumably to borrow some coats. Alerted to what had happened at Little Bohemia, the Koerners had notified the Feds.

The late Tom Hollatz, local author of the book *Gangster Holidays, the Lore and Legends of the Badguys,* relates in an interview years later with Wanatka's son, Emil Jr., as to what happened after Wanatka arrived at Koerners:

Baby Face forced my father to drive, sitting next to him. The car choked, and Nelson became madder. Just then a car turned in from the highway. The car carried two FBI men and the local constable. When he couldn't move any further (the way blocked by the other car) Baby Face jumped out to confront the startled agents and Constable Christensen. That's when my father jumped out of the car and rolled over a high snow bank to get away.

At this point Nelson began firing into the car. All three wounded agents managed to get out of the car, but Carter Baum died by a fence 40 feet away. Constable Christensen collapsed nearby and Jay Newman escaped through the woods.

Nelson took the agent's car and headed for the back roads. The two main highways, 70 and 13, were now under guard.

He didn't get far before developing car trouble, so he started to walk. It was a long cold hike, but by dawn he had arrived in Lac du Flambeau on the Ojibwe reservation. He stayed for a couple of days at a cabin just outside of town with a man named Ollie Catfish. (That cabin is available for rent at what is known today as Dillman's Sand Lake Lodge.) Nelson traded clothes with Catfish for a couple of days before stealing a local mailman's car and heading to St. Paul.

The gang molls, among them Helen Gillis, were arrested at Little Bo. Gillis was paroled after three weeks in a Chicago jail. She joined up with her husband who had found his way back to the city by that time.

After John Dillinger was shot down outside the Chicago theatre, both John Hamilton and Homer Van Meter were killed. Other gangsters of the time, *Pretty Boy* Floyd and Bonnie and Clyde, had also bitten the dust!

Baby Face, who had hoped to organize a new gang, would soon find out that his buddies Eddie Green and Tommy Carroll had been killed. So, along with John Paul Chase and Helen, he headed back to California, and then Nevada, where they stayed for a few months.

Baby Face, now "Public Enemy No. 1" on the FBI list, knew that he did not live up to the perceived notoriety of the infamous Dillinger. Maybe he should start robbing banks...! But nobody wanted to play bank robber with Nelson. He was too well known and way too hot-headed.

The feds were after "No. 1" and knew he frequented places in Lake Geneva just over the Wisconsin border. Having failed at one stakeout area, FBI inspector Samuel Crowley stepped up his surveillance. Agents were on area roads from dawn to sunset, and lingered at rest stops and diners hoping to spot the Nelsons or Chase.

Then, on November 27, 1934 agents spotted Nelson (along with his wife and Chase) in a stolen car heading south on their way to Barrington, Illinois. Other accounts say Nelson spotted the agents, turned around, and followed them, eventually disabling the government car's radiator. Then a second government car arrived on the scene carrying Crowley and Herman Hollis. But whether there were two cars or one, and regardless of who chased whom, the outcome is not disputed.

Nelson approached the agents firing steadily from his machine gun, killing both Crowley and Hollis. But the return shots had taken their toll as well. The Public Enemy No. 1 title would have to go to someone else.

Chase drove the government car away from the scene. Helen wrapped her husband's body in a blanket. "He always hated being cold," she supposedly lamented. The body was left in a ditch across from a Catholic cemetery in Skokie, Illinois. Agents found it the next day. Nelson and his wife are both buried at St. Joseph's Cemetery in River Grove, Illinois.

Reportedly, the ghost of Lester Gillis is sometimes spotted on streets of the seedy side of Reno, "the biggest little city in the world." Or maybe that ghost is really the spirit of Roy Frisch who is still trying to testify against the underworld figures.

Regardless, I have never heard stories of any Gillis ghosts in the Northwoods. But then, he didn't spend as much time up here as, say, the Capone brothers. Maybe Baby Face found it too frigid and snowy here in the winter! He never did like the cold!

CHAPTER 4

BLAZING RED JACKET

**The piano played a slow funeral tune
And the town was lit up
by the cold Christmas moon
The parents they cried
and the miners they moaned
Oh see what your greed for money has done[4]**

In this last stanza Woody Guthrie summarizes the *Nineteen Thirteen Massacre* in Calumet, Michigan (located on the west side of the Keweenaw Peninsula about 20 miles north of Houghton).

It was Christmas Eve and the families of striking miners gathered on the second floor of the Italian Benevolent Society Hall to attend a party sponsored by the Western Federation of Miners. About 700 union members and their families were in attendance.

But, before relating *the rest of the story*, a little more background....

Copper was actually mined in the Peninsula as early as 5,000 to 1,000 B.C. Much later (1660) Jesuit missionaries arrived here to look for the precious metal.

---

[4] Verse from "Nineteen Thirteen Massacre," Woody Guthrie 1941

Calumet was settled in 1864, originally named Red Jacket after the copper mine there of the same name. The mine, in turn, was named after American Indian Chief Red Jacket of the Seneca tribe of the Iroquois Nation who received his name from an embroidered red coat given to him by the British for his support in the American Revolution. The chief sided with the Americans during the War of 1812.

I am not really sure what the connection is to the Chief and the Red Jacket Mine; i.e., why the mine was so named since the Seneca Tribe was located in New York. The only reference of the Senecas being in Michigan that I could find was the following from the book *Indian Names in Michigan* by Virgil J. Vogel:

> In 1662 an Iroquois war party of 100 encamped on the shore of Whitefish Bay of Lake Superior, in present Chippewa country, only a few miles west of Sault St. Marie. They were soon discovered by an equally numerous band of Ojibwa, Ottawa and allied Indians, who made a surprise attack that annihilated the invaders. The Iroquois never again tried to advance into Ojibwa territory.

But, for whatever reason, the town was so named. Red Jacket was incorporated in 1867. A neighboring town was named Calumet. Calumet became Laurium in 1895. Red Jacket became Calumet in 1929. If that is confusing to you, never mind, The above-mentioned information is just a result of my trivial pursuit!

In 1871 the Calumet and Hecla mining companies merged into the largest copper mining company in Michigan (later known as C&H). Job seekers came from all over Europe and Asia including Finland, Great Britain, Poland, Hungary, Austria, Croatia, Germany, Italy, and even Greece and China.

Miners armed with drills and sledgehammers (and hot pasties for their lunch) descended into the 600-foot-deep mines each day for a salary of $2.75 per 12-hour day. A few earned up to $4 per day! Workers toiled ten hours a day six days of the week. Depths of certain mine shafts in the Calumet area approached a mile.

The Calumet Conglomerate was the Mother Lode. Over half of the nation's copper was produced here between 1871 and 1880. During its heyday, the township of Calumet boasted a population of over 100,000 and was known for its wild-west frontier lifestyle. Over 70 saloons dotted the town. On the other hand, every ethnic group had a church; there were six Catholic churches alone.

In 1901 James MacNaughton became general manager of the Calumet & Hecla mines. The mine management in Boston felt the miners at C&H needed more control and less pampering. MacNaughton hated unions and would not hire anyone with a union background. He brought in spies and detectives to keep a finger on the climate.

Despite his efforts, the Western Federation of Miners union began to organize workers in the area in 1909. While wages were competitive, they were subject to whims of management. Wages might be lowered during a downturn in sales or even as new equipment was introduced.

Conditions in the mines were abhorrent. In 1912 alone, forty-seven men were killed while working in mines and over 600 seriously injured (Nearly 4,000 more received slight injuries.) Add to that the fact that the mines were damp, dusty, and unsanitary. There were no lavatories; men simply relieved themselves wherever they were working.

The Company owned the town. They leased land to workers to build homes on. If a miner was fired or failed to meet the terms of the vague and unclear lease, the Company could obtain ownership of the house on the leased property. Home rental contracts could be terminated the same way—for no particular reason. Workers who sued the company usually quit, because they would be fired if they didn't.

One of the longest strikes in the area's history began July 23, 1913 and included all of the C&H mines. A new drilling system had been implemented in the mines. A one-man drilling system replaced the three-man system (actually called the "two-man drill"). While reducing costs, introduction of the new mechanical drills resulted in many layoffs. Add to that wage issues and less-than-desirable working conditions, and approximately 16,000 Western Federation of Miners (WFM) men struck 21 mines— nine of them C&H mines.

National Guard cavalrymen, with their machine guns, were sent in to control the picketers. The Waddell-Mahon detective agency provided hundreds of gunmen, spies, and thugs. Over 1,000 strikers were beaten, arrested and jailed. Outside strikebreakers were brought in, held under armed guard and forced to work.

August 14, 1913 was the date of the first strike-related killings. Two striking miners had left a mine office near Painesdale (south of Houghton) after checking on their strike benefits. They walked down a path they always took towards their home. A deputized mine employee ordered them to stop and turn back. The men felt they did not have to obey a mine supervisor since they were no longer employed. A Waddell security agent watched while the two men headed down the path. He called in five other agents and approached one of the men as he arrived at his boarding house. One agent grabbed the man and said "I want you." A struggle ensued and they began to beat him with clubs. Roommates came out of the house and joined in the fracas. One threw a bowling pin, but missed his target. The agent turned and fired his gun, killing a man standing in the doorway of the house. The agents then ran inside the house firing their guns until they ran out of ammunition. Another man inside the house was killed. Others, including a baby, were injured. The agents then scattered empty bottles in the yard to make it seem like the men in the boarding house had started the fight. There was never an attempt to arrest anyone.

Then on September 2, nearly 200 striking workers, as well as women and children, protested in the streets. They were confronted by several deputized men. A verbal exchanged ensued, and the deputies fired into the unarmed crowd, hitting a teenage girl in the head. The girl did recover, but it was another incident of violence leading up to the massacre at Italian Hall.

Brutality continued; strikers were severely beaten at the slightest provocation. New workers arrived from Germany, never told that there was a strike in progress. Unreasonable contracts (in English) were given to the men to sign. Six of the 37 Germans left the train to the mines when they found out they had been deceived. The others were held captive and escorted by Waddell's men to the mine. Armed agents were sent to round up the escaped Germans.

Gunshots, and even bomb threats, were common. Then, on December 6, rounds of bullets from two high-powered rifles were shot into another boarding house in Painesdale. Two men from Great Britain were killed instantly.

Around this same time the Citizens' Alliance was formed. Although the Alliance was said to be comprised of a nonpartisan group of citizens and businessmen who wanted an end to the strike, it was really a group of mining company supporters who signed a pledge to defeat and abolish the WFM. Every member was required to wear the round white button with big red letters proclaiming Citizens Alliance membership.

Aroused by mine management by allegations and propaganda, the Alliance became a bit out of control. They vandalized buildings, raided union headquarters, and threatened union members if they did not leave town.

So now the stage has been set for the Christmas party held the afternoon of December 24, 1913.

Striking miners and their families arrived at a WFM-sponsored Christmas party held on the second floor of the "Societa Mutua Beneficenza Italiana" (Italian Mutual Benefit Society). Everyone called the building "Italian Hall." There was a saloon and an Atlantic & Pacific Tea Co. store on the main floor. The main hall, where the party was held, was on the second floor, accessed by a stairway at the left of the building.

The majority of the estimated 700 party-goers were children. Union sympathizers throughout the country donated gifts for the function. The Women's Auxiliary collected money from merchants. Two trees were decorated. There were no candles on the trees because of a fire risk. It was to be a night of singing and dancing, fun and food, an escape from the stressful lives of the striking miners. A ballerina performed. Saffron cake was served, and there were barrels of chocolate drops for the children.

Photo in Coppertown Mining Museum
Calumet, MI

]

The children seemed to be eager for their presents, The program was shortened a bit so that they might make their way to the stage. After they received their gifts, some children left the party. Most, however, stayed on while their families visited with friends and relatives. The noise level was high. Women on stage could scarcely make their announcements.

Woody Guthrie's song continues:

> **Talking and laughing is heard everywhere**
> **And the spirit of Christmas is there in the air**
> **Before you know it you're friends with us all**
> **And you're dancing around and around in the hall**

People were enjoying themselves. But the party was about to turn ugly.

> **A little girl sits down by the Christmas tree lights**
> **To play the piano, so you've got to keep quiet**
> **To hear all this fun you would not realize**
> **That the copper boss thug–men are milling outside**

Suddenly, a man wearing a dark coat and a hat pulled low over his eyes entered the hall. He loudly yelled "Fire," and then quickly ran down the stairs and outside of the building.

The crowd panicked and rushed for the steep staircase, the only obvious exit from their upstairs room. (There was a poorly-marked fire escape where ladders could be accessed by climbing through the windows, but it was not noticed in the panic.) One woman on stage tried to yell "There is no fire." Her voice was drowned out by the screams and noise of people rushing for the stairs.

Copper boss thugs stick their heads in the door
One of them yelled, and he screamed There's a fire
A lady she hollered, There's no such a thing
Keep on with your dancing there's no such a thing

A few people rushed, but it was only a few
It's just the scabs and the thugs fooling you
A man grabbed his daughter and carried her down
But the thugs held the door
and they could not get out

The first party-goers to reach the doors found they couldn't open them. Behind them people stumbled and fell. As they pushed and shoved, more fell and were crushed by the crowd.

The saloon keeper from the tavern on the first floor climbed a ladder to the upper floor and helped rescue workers. When he returned to his saloon, he found that his till had been robbed and much of his stock of liquor gone.

Outside of the building deputies were attempting to keep people looking for family members out of the building. Shoving matches broke out; deputies clubbed people they couldn't control.

Seventy-three people were smothered in the staircase. Approximately two thirds of them were children. There was no fire. The individual who yelled "Fire" was never identified. Many said that he was wearing a Citizens Alliance pin. Perhaps that person was only trying to spoil the party as just another routine provocation against the strikers. Or the result might have been the culmination of his plan. Regardless, the outcome was definitely disastrous.

Interestingly, another fire alarm was called into the station just 45 minutes after the Italian Hall alarm. It was a call for a chimney fire at the McNaughton house in Hecla.

The funeral cortege was two miles long. Miners carried the white coffins containing the children. Adults were buried in black coffins.

Original doors of Italian Hall
Displayed at Coppertown Mining Museum

The Citizen's Alliance visited Charles Moyer, president of the WFM, on Christmas Day. They offered $25,000 in relief funds. He grudgingly replied, "The WFM will bury its own dead."

The following day several Citizens Alliance members were accompanied by Sheriff Cruse (an Alliance ally) to the hotel where head of the union, Charles

Moyer, was staying. The group demanded that Moyer retract any and all statements he had made that blamed the Alliance for the tragedy. He refused.

Shortly thereafter, a mob of about twenty entered Moyer's room and began beating him. Someone hit him in the back of the head with a handgun. It discharged, lodging a bullet in Moyer's shoulder. They then dragged him from his hotel and to the train station. Two Alliance members boarded the train with Moyer to ensure his destination would be Chicago.

Confusion prevailed in the aftermath of the tragedy. A coroner's inquest was held with a jury selected by the coroner who was appointed by The Houghton County Board of Commissioners. Most members of the Board were from mining companies or businesses dependent upon the industry. Many, including McNaughton, were mine managers. The coroner selected his jury, so one could assume that the members would be pro-Citizens Alliance. In fact, nine of them were actually Citizens Alliance members.

The jury members were sworn in the night of the tragedy. Hearings began on December 29 and lasted only three days. Although many witnesses had identified the man who shouted "Fire" as wearing a white Citizens Alliance button on his coat, newspapers declared on the first day of the inquest that the person did NOT have an Alliance button on. When asked the question of a button, witnesses often replied "I don't know." So, when asked the next question "Did you see one?" The obvious answer was "No."

There was uncertainty as to whether all members attending the party were asked to show their union card. Many said it was loosely controlled and that a Citizens Alliance member certainly could have slipped in, if only momentarily.

Other problems with the inquest include the fact that many of the immigrants spoke only broken English. Without interpreters, they could not understand some of the questions or express themselves accurately. Some answers needed clarification, yet jurors did not ask further questions. And, there was no mention made as to which way the doors at the bottom of the stairs opened.

Though many believed that the doors opened inwardly toward the stairs, pictures seemed to show that they opened toward the street. Inside the building was another set of doors. Originally thought to open inwardly, later examination of clearer photos showed the opposite to be true. And, there simply wasn't room for them to open towards the stairs. (The door controversy came later; nobody at the time claimed that the doors opened inwardly.)

Though the people killed that Christmas Eve were trampled and smothered as they stumbled and fell in the stairwell, a long-standing debate continued over whether the doors (opening inwardly) caused the deaths, or whether thugs or members of the Citizens Alliance actually held the doors closed, preventing escape. Woody Guthrie and Bob Dylan believe the latter theory.

The United States Congress came to the Keweenaw Peninsula to investigate conditions relating to mining, the strike, National Guard conduct...and the Italian Hall tragedy. They hired translators, and delved into issues—unlike the jury at the coroner's inquest.

As mentioned, the man who yelled fire was identified as having the Citizens Alliance button on his coat. Also, it was agreed that he had a hat pulled low on his face and sported a mustache. They said he made his appearance in the Hall at an entrance near the stage, having come up the stairs leading from the street (opposite the entrance that the party-goers used). After yelling "Fire," the man ran out of the Hall, down the stairs and into the street. One witness claimed to have seen the man earlier, on the streets carrying a club—like a deputy or a security man.

Some who were at the Hall that afternoon recalled the man who yelled "Fire" as having a little can from which he sprinkled something, maybe a slippery substance so people would fall on the stairs. Some believed it may have been poison gas.

Some survivors reached conclusions from past experiences or present observations. Mine workers were familiar with the dangers of natural gas or carbon monoxide, and even smoke, in the enclosed mine shafts. Some who viewed the bodies after the tragedy at Italian Hall remember seeing no signs of injury; many died with their eyes open. And it seemed probable to some that people piled at the bottom of the stairs might have slipped on the stairs and tumbled to the bottom. From perceptions came rumors, then beliefs.

In 1975 there was an effort by various groups in the Calumet area to preserve the Italian Hall. The U.S.

Park Service sent in a man to evaluate the deteriorating structure. The inspector reported the double doors at the bottom of the stairs opened inwardly!

Regardless, the real cause of the incident was the man who yelled "Fire," right? Yet, many witnesses in a hearing held by the United States Congress' House Committee investigation in February 1914 claimed that they did not hear anyone yell "Fire."

Perceptions, emotions and conspiracy blended with facts and rationalization. Today, even the number of deaths from the terrible incident is not a fixed figure.

The original Italian Hall, a wood building, burned down on New Year's Eve 1907. A brick building was built in its place the following year. (Note: Local newspapers of the time reported updates described doors that swung outwards.)

The building was demolished in 1984. The archway that held the doors sits in the middle of Memorial Park, on the lot where the Hall once stood. Behind the arch is a photo of the Hall. A historical marker tells of the tragedy, but says that it was partially caused by doors that opened inwardly!

What information, and which people, can we believe? I believe, as does the author of *Death's Door*, Steve Lehto, that someone did yell "Fire," maybe to disrupt the party or harass the miners and their families. Perhaps he was as shocked as anyone when 73 men, women and children died that evening.

Even if the doors opened outwardly, the narrow stairway and rushing crowds resulted in people stumbling and falling over bodies as they tried to reach safety. People were suffocated and trampled, and the stairwell was eventually blocked with a mass of people.

Archway that once housed the entrance doors to Italian Hall

The cover-ups and untruths spread by papers like the *Calumet News* tried to protect the reputation of mine management. But one fact remains: Not a soul was charged for any wrongdoing. Despite a couple of stories of men confessing on their death bed that they had gone upstairs into the auditorium and cried "Fire," those stories were judged not to be credible.

Some say that on quiet nights one can hear the cries of children; their wails seem to emanate from the arch. Their innocent souls transcend the hatred, the violence and the discrimination heaped upon their families. Their young lives were snuffed out by what was believed at the time to be a blaze, but in reality was only a bluff.

CHAPTER 5

SUMMERWIND

**I dwell in a lonely house I know
That vanished many a summer ago,
And left no trace but the cellar walls,
And a cellar in which the daylight falls...[5]**

I had been down that county road so many times. Little did I know that I was only a mile or two from the ruins of what was once a massive grand mansion—with a very interesting, and terrifying, history!

The building that would come to be known as Summerwind was constructed as a fishing lodge in the early 1900s. Robert Lamont bought the property in 1916 and transformed it into a magnificent home for his family. Nestled in a clearing of pine trees overlooking West Bay Lake in northern Wisconsin, it was only a couple of miles off the main road, yet isolated enough to provide the utmost seclusion and privacy.

West Bay Lake is one of a chain of fifteen lakes in the Cisco Chain of Lakes. Most of the lakes lie in the Upper Peninsula of Michigan just west of Watersmeet, but a few like West Bay Lake extend down into Wisconsin. Summerwind was a stone's

---

[5] Verse from "Ghost House," Robert Frost

throw from the border. What promised to be the perfect escape from the chaos and commotion of Chicago and Washington D.C. to a peaceful dream home in the Northwoods would become a nightmare for the Lamonts and subsequent owners as well—a true House of Horrors!

Robert Lamont

Michigan native Robert Patterson Lamont succeeded Herbert Hoover as Secretary of Commerce in 1929 when Hoover became President of the United States. Lamont left that position in 1932 and went back to Chicago to become president of the American Iron and Steel Institute.

There were rumors of illegal activities and cover-ups during the 1920 Census in the capacity Lamont performed prior to his Secretary appointment. Lamont supposedly later remarked that he "was haunted by the twice dead" a remark some attributed to removing names of voters from polling lists and listing as them as deceased.

So, maybe this is where the ghost stories started, but one event that happened early on at Lamont's Summerwind seems to be widely circulated, and pictures taken years later seemed to verify it. As Lamont was sitting at the kitchen table with his wife, the nearby door to the basement opened and an apparition appeared. Frightened, Lamont grabbed his pistol and fired at the ghost. By that time it had disappeared and slammed the door shut.

Lucy of Lilac Hills

Local author, the late Tom Hollatz, told a story of Robert Lamont in his book *The Haunted Northwoods* published in 2000. He gained the following information from an interview with a lady named Emily Warren from Ohio who said she spent her childhood summers at West Bay Lake.

I cannot find any verification of some of the specifics that Emily presents, such as the mansion being called "Lilac Hills." Though I have never seen mention of that name connected to "Summerwind," there is a haunted home built in 1832 in Fayette, Missouri called Lilac Hills.

Also, my sources state that Robert Patterson Lamont married Gertrude Trotter in 1867, and they had three children: Robert Jr., Dorothy and Gertrude. The only mention of a Lucy Devereau (mentioned by Emily) that I could find was a mysterious detective character in a book called "The Darkening" by Chandler McGrew.

Regardless, the following story that was told to Hollatz by Emily is interesting to say the least.

Back in the lean times following the Civil War many wealthy plantation owners "found themselves facing ruin." In many cases the estates were deserted and the family moved on. Slaves were freed or frequently sold. Daughters of plantation owners sometimes were sold too, or forced into marriage. Such was the case of Lucy Devereau, daughter of the owner of Whitehall Plantation near Atlanta. Reportedly, Lucy was a mistress of the senior Robert Lamont, but agreed to marry his son (Robert Patterson Lamont) in order to save the family plantation.

Lucy embedded herself in New York's high society and was not thrilled when her husband decided to move to a far-off wilderness with a totally different lifestyle. But move they, did along with her servant, Hannah.

The West Bay Lake home was lavishly decorated and furnished with antiques purchased in their travels abroad. But Lucy missed the big city.

After she brought a son, James, into the world, Lucy seemed more content—for a while. But Robert controlled virtually all of Lucy's activities. She had no friends and was not allowed to leave the mansion. She was even discouraged from talking to people who happened their way.

Lucy eventually had another child, a daughter named after her who died shortly after birth. Baby Lucy purportedly is buried on the property.

Lucy became more despondent. Her letters to her family in Georgia told of screams in the night and voices—though no one was there. Then her son James began to behave strangely. The mansion was haunted; she had to find a way to escape!

She managed to befriend an employee of her husband, a man named John Wittington. On a cold November day Lucy, John, James and Hannah escaped to Ontonagon on the shores of Lake Superior. From there they headed to Georgia where Lucy hoped to reunite with her family. Her resourceful husband caught up with the four of them in Virginia and brought Lucy back to Wisconsin.

Young Emily and her friends at the lake would visit Summerwind after it had been vacated. Many times the group would take shelter there when a storm would whip up over the lake. Often they would see the woman who resembled the painting above the fireplace. She always appeared to be wearing a long white gown. And though her eyes looked sad, she would smile at the children and then disappear.

Then, one day, as they were climbing the hill up to the house, Lucy's ghost appeared on the porch frantically motioning the children to get down. Just then shots were fired over their heads. The caretaker was drunk and was shooting from the porch out onto the lake.

Several accounts from this version just do not ring true with me. But, with some assumptions about the age of Emily and the various times the mansion was vacant, the recollections could certainly "fit" into Summerwind's timeline. Emily probably would have heard stories of the Lamont family from someone older than she.

The Hinshaws

Sometime in the mid 30s, shortly after Lamont shot at the apparition, the family apparently left their summer home for good. In the 1940s the property was sold to the Keefer family who apparently never lived in the home. Robert Lamont died in 1948. The Hinshaws bought the mansion in the early 1970s. It is with their residence that the ghost stories proliferated!

Shadows appeared in hallways. Soft voices ceased talking when someone walked into a room. Windows opened and closed. An apparition of a woman floated throughout the home. The children had encounters with ghosts too. Hired men refused to do any more work on the house, so the Hinshaws started to remodel on their own.

(Note: It is a common occurrence that during periods of renovation on a building, paranormal activities seem to spike; i.e., during building days, the spirits will play!)

At Summerwind, the *play* seemed to be anything but...something more sinister was involved. Arnold Hinshaw found a hidden crevice behind a closet drawer. Upon further inspection, the recess was found to contain a human corpse. Another time, his automobile suddenly burst into flames. Arnold started to pound the keys of their piano late at night, like a frenzied madman. He eventually suffered a breakdown and was hospitalized for treatment. Ginger Hinshaw attempted suicide and went to live with her parents in southern Wisconsin. The couple later divorced. And Summerwind reverted to Mrs. Keefer.

Ray Bober and Carver's Deed

Ginger remarried, this time to a man named George Olsen. A few years later Ginger was faced with a big surprise. Her father, Ray Bober and his wife planned to purchase Summerwind and turn it into an inn. Seems they had no knowledge of what had happened there to Ginger. Ray knew of ghost stories there, but was not afraid. In fact, he claimed to know who the ghost was: Jonathan Carver, a British explorer. Bober believed that Carver was looking for a land deed that he assumed was buried at Summerwind. Bober believed Carver was angry because he could not find his deed. He claimed that

Carver's apparition asked him to help find the document. Bober even chipped out holes in the foundation looking for it, but never found anything.

Jonathan Carver found his way into Wisconsin and lived with the Dakota Indians in 1766-77. In May of 1977 Carver received a large land grant from the Dakotas but died without getting his grant ratified by the King of England. A 1763 Proclamation of the King of Britain said that private persons could not purchase land from Indians. Perhaps Carver thought that because the land was awarded outside of Britain, the proclamation did not apply. Supposedly the Carver heirs had the deed in their possession and sold their land grants to Mr. and Mrs. Houghton in 1794. Even at that, the U. S. Congress had passed the first of Trade and Intercourse acts allowing only fur traders onto Indian territories and declared privately acquired lands from Indians invalid. (But how would the ghost Carver know that? Carver died in 1780, ten years before the above act was passed!)

Another question remains: Why would Carver's ghost be looking for his lost deed at Summerwind? According to a map plotted by historian John G. Gregory, the land grant extended only to Manitowish, some forty miles west of Summerwind.

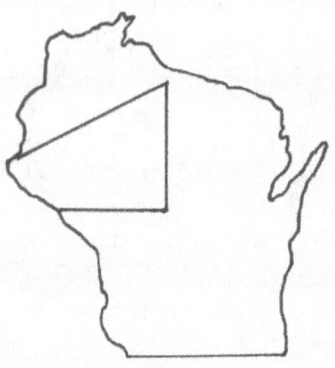

Map by John Gregory shows triangle assumed to be land deeded to explorer Jonathan Carter. Land is bordered by the Mississippi River, Pittsville, Manitowish, and a spot near St. Paul, Minnesota.

Strange happenings continued to occur at Summerwind. Shortly after he purchased the home, Bober, son Karl, along with Ginger and George, drove up to Summerwind and went through the house. George looked in the closet and found the crevice where the skeleton was found years before, but there were no bones there now! He had not known of the skeleton, but Ginger told the rest of the family everything later that day.

Later that summer, Karl came back to the property to do some work. Alone in the house, he heard someone call his name. He closed the upstairs window and headed down the steps. As he walked into the front room, he heard two loud shots. He walked into the smoke-filled room, but nobody was there. The only bullet holes he found were those made years ago in the basement door by Robert Lamont.

Workmen again left their jobs. Their tools would be missing. Measurements taken one day would change greatly the next day. The house seemed to be larger than the blueprint measurements and later return to the original size.

Ray's wife, Marie, had experiences too. At times she felt that someone was following her. Marie took photographs of the living room. There were no curtains hanging when she took the photos (Ginger had taken them down when she left the home), yet curtains appeared on the developed pictures.

The Bobers always slept in their RV parked in the yard; they never spent a night inside Summerwind! Eventually they gave up their plans for an inn and abandoned the property. Bober would later write a book published in 1979 entitled, *The Carver Effect* under the pen name of Wolfgang von Bober.

The Demise of Summerwind

In 1985, after her husband Lou died and she was sole owner of the 120 acre parcel of property that Summerwind was built on, Lillian Keefer subdivided the land to various purchasers.

Summerwind was deserted much of the 1980s. In 1986 Walter and Berniece Petgas took ownership of the property. In June 1988 Summerwind burned to the ground after being struck by lightning during a fierce storm.

Others will say it was burned down by locals who did not like the frequent visits by thrill seekers or partiers. Town Chairman Ronald Ramesh supposedly wanted to petition for a burning permit before townspeople learned about their plans. He was "worried that a save-the-mansion movement would erupt when the word got out.")

More stories surfaced during the '80s from people who visited the crumbling Summerwind. Stories of exorcisms, and incidents predicted by Ouija boards: a heavy tile blowing through a window and striking the head of a board player; visitors having a car accident on their way home that ended in a death of the man driving the other car; orders to LEAVE: the message from Jonathan Carver! One time a cold beer can suddenly appeared on a concrete railing. Photos, when developed, showed orbs and misty images.

Judy Dietz, Manitowish Waters, recalls a visit to Summerwind with her husband in recent years. It was a windy day, but as they reached the road into the old mansion, the air was suddenly, eerily still. Judy's heart began to pound; something told her to stay away. The feeling was strong—as if she would be under some hex if she disobeyed her instincts. While her husband explored the ruins, she remained in the driveway. Then, as they left the property, the wind picked up as to escort them down the road and away from the haunted estate.

Sisters Becky and Heidi Rattenbach first visited Summerwind in the early 1980s after a camping trip near Lake Superior. On the way back, another friend said "You gotta see this place." That very night they visited Summerwind.

From that night until just before Summerwind burned down, they visited the haunted estate regularly (went back to their *old haunts*, so to speak). Although they didn't have a supernatural experience every time they visited, enough happened that they became firm believers.

Becky initiated our conversation with the statement "I believe in ghosts." To that Heidi added, "All those things you read on the internet about Summerwind...they're true!"

They described the property. There were three major buildings: the home, the maids' quarters and the butlers' quarters. (They found it interesting that the maids' quarters consisted of one big room with multiple beds, while there were private rooms in the butlers' quarters, and fireplaces too.)

A gate to the estate had bullet holes in it. On a visit two days later they noticed the holes were not there. Their car radio would not work as they approached or departed Summerwind. Once they were off the property, it worked just fine.

"We had to take the keys out of the car door or the doors would be locked when we came to leave." (This was before power locks when "you had to lock each door separately.")

Becky lamented, "I wish I still had my pictures." Apparently she loaned them to someone who didn't return them. She went on to tell of one photograph taken outside the home that showed a wall half stained; a vertical line came through and separated it from the other half that was not stained. Actually, the outside walls were completely stained.

On one particular stormy night there was a flash of lightening. The dark windows suddenly appeared to be boarded up.

Rooms would "be there one time and not the next." Dimension would change. Heidi described the fireplace. "It was beautiful, with turquoise stones." The next time they visited, it wasn't there.

Becky (left) and Heidi Rattenbach

I had to ask the question; both women adamantly denied that they did any drinking or anything else that would alter their minds! Another thing they would not do during their visits was to take a Ouji board onto the property.

Although they didn't communicate to each other when it happened, there was something else. To the left of the fireplace was a stairway with an open door. "A black figure" described as a "dark mist" went up the stairs. I asked if they would characterize this figure as male or female. They believed it to be the former.

There was a female ghost too. They wondered if she was the lady who hung herself in the house. I asked who that was, remembering that Ginger Hinshaw tried to commit suicide. They didn't know.

In the basement newspapers dated 1932 were found. While the group looked around with a flashlight, Heidi turned around—a noose was hanging directly in front of her face. They noticed a "huge boiler" in the basement. Two days later they came back; it was gone.

A hallway door was open, closed a bit, then slammed shut. There was absolutely no wind blowing through the house. Becky remembers, "I didn't stop running until we got out of there."

An American Indian friend offered tobacco. It was sprinkled under a tree as an offering to the spirits to ensure peace. But there would be no serenity at Summerwind.

Buddy, an acquaintance of the Rattenbachs, "lost control of his own mind." Buddy believed someone was calling him back to the house. He began speaking in tongues. Finally, he was taken to a priest in Boulder Junction for an exorcism.

Nothing must be removed from Summerwind. Those who took items often had, to put it mildly, bad luck. A friend removed a brick from the property; he broke his ankle a week later. Another person took a cook stove. He divorced, and then died of kidney failure. Were these events coincidences? Perhaps, we will never know.

The women returned to Summerwind until the year it burned down. But it was a bit strange, they remembered. Though Summerwind was completely destroyed by fire, not one of the dry trees right next to the house caught afire.

My Search

I moved to the Northwoods in 1997 and shortly thereafter began to hear stories about the haunted mansion. It wasn't until May 2009 when I decided I had to find the site, feel the history, and walk the grounds that spirits are said to still roam today. I didn't have any delusions that I would be possessed or any such thing; I have long believed that I just don't have the capabilities to experience psychic and paranormal occurrences. Ghosts may not reveal themselves to me, but my interest certainly is present!

First I had to *find* Summerwind. Google provided me with a pretty good map, but I knew from previous accounts that this property would be difficult to locate. I hijacked my husband, and we made a day out of it. We went out for breakfast in Land O' Lakes, then crossed into Michigan where we spent a little time at the Lac Vieux Desert casino. After donating a bit of money there, we backtracked to Land O' Lakes and west to Helen Creek Road off County B. I didn't have high hopes, but we were rewarded after just one wrong fork in the road. We turned around at a dead end with power lines in view. As we went back and took another road, we saw a driveway.

It didn't look like an actual driveway, but we could tell people had driven that way! We continued on this bumpy, grassy drive up a small hill. And as we crested—THERE IT WAS: SUMMERWIND! What a thrill!

The foundation and chimneys are all that remain.

Blood-red graffiti scrawled at the cave's entrance.

Today the property is owned by Harold Tracy of Chicago. Phone calls to his home go unanswered.

The ghosts of Summerwind seem to be resting. Perhaps if a home is ever rebuilt here, and the spirits feel the intrusion of their quiet space, we may hear more stories. Hopefully the ghosts will be of a kinder, gentler nature and there will be no more death and destruction. Until then, the impressive ruins remain on the crest of the wooded hillside overlooking West Bay Lake. They silently greet the changing seasons, and open their aging arms to the soft and sultry summer winds!

I am reminded of verses from the song that Frank Sinatra crooned so many years ago:*

> The summer wind, came blowin' in
> From across the sea
> It lingered there, so warm and fair
> To walk with me...
>
> The autumn wind
> And the winter wind
> Have come and gone
> And still the days, those lonely days
> Go on and on....*

You are not going to believe this, but I just heard a doorbell ring. There was nobody at the door; in fact I don't have a doorbell! I think it came from within my computer. Perhaps it was Jonathon Carver ringing the bell of the door that was once the entrance to Summerwind. Come in, Mr. Carver.... No one is there; I guess I just *mist* him!

---

* Verses from "Summer Winds," Henry Mayer and Johnny Mercer 1965

70

CHAPTER 6

STRAWBERRY SPIRITS

This bank, in which the dead were laid,
Was sacred when its soil was ours;
Hither the artless Indian maid
Brought wreaths of beads and flowers,
And the gray chief and gifted seer
Worshipped the god of thunders here.[6]

We met Ray Raychel when he signed up to take the real estate law class that my husband taught out of our home. Ray had moved to the Minocqua, Wisconsin area from the southern part of the state. Soon after our meeting, we first heard about Strawberry Island.

Prior to bringing his wife to the Minocqua area, Ray came alone--with his boat, a tent and camping gear. He explored the area a bit, pitching his tent wherever his explorations ended for the day. Vilas County is home to over 1,300 lakes, one of the most concentrated areas of lake in the world, including several *chains*. One such chain of lakes is located in Lac du Flambeau, a beautiful string of ten lakes stretching from Pokegama Lake at the northern end to Fence Lake on the southeastern side.

---

[6] Verse from "An Indian at the Burial Place of His Fathers, William Cullen Bryant.

71

It was at a boat landing on Fence Lake that Ray loaded his camping gear and launched his 18' runabout. From here he traveled into Crawling Stone Lake, then Interlaken. He was ready to settle in for the evening when he spotted a large heavily forested island on Flambeau Lake. The cool October night would bring a real chill to Ray's overnight camping trip.

Ray Raychel recalls his camping outing.

Following is Ray's written version of the night he spent on Strawberry Island:

It was October; early in this transition month as the calendar would indicate, but late in these waning days of this Autumn Season. Warm and Sunny, Cool and Calm, Chilling and Windy. It was all of these combinations...a worthy time for a contemplative getaway. The trip's planning had been completed; the mode had been determined. This would be an escape from the normality of everyday: a Lewis and Clark expedition on a wilderness water trip.

Spanning a chain of lakes in the beautiful Northwoods of Wisconsin, my journey would begin on the most southern end of the Fence lake Chain of Lakes on the reservation known as Lac Du Flambeau (or Lake of the Torches as Native American heritage had appointed it).

My travels that first day went according to plan, and I arrived at the north side of Strawberry Island on Flambeau Lake just before dusk would approach. I moored my boat about 15 feet offshore as the rocks and obstacles near the shoreline seemed to warn me to keep off. Thinking nothing of this, as the water was only 1-2 feet deep at this location, I secured my boat with two anchors; one in the water and one on the shore. As the trip's duty suggested, my first task would be to explore. Wading through the now chilly water up to the island, I had to climb a short hill to reach the top. Here I found a campsite, full with a rock fire pit, sticks and logs aplenty to make a fire and some even ground for a bed near the fire. Surely, I had not been the first to inhabit this particular spot. Convenient I thought, timesaving for sure, as the needed amenities would make this first nights adventure easier.

Hurrying back to the boat before darkness became established, I retrieved my camp stove, sleeping bag, and food for the evening meal. Campfire ignited and a quick meal accomplished, I headed for my resting place for the evening.

As I settled down for my first night's rest, the breezes seemed to carry sounds, unexplainable to my knowledge of this Indian site. Gunshots? Or was it simply trees breaking under the pressure on the winds of the night. Voices groaning? Or was it the nocturnal calls of some animal inhabitants of the island. Battle cries of tribes long gone? Or was it just the mixture of sounds carried by the winds from nearby communities. My mind raced with fear and warning that the darkness would yield, yet my sleep was relaxed as the solitude of my location would yield to the weary.

When the drums started to beat the rhythms of long ago native ceremonies, the voices of tongues not understood and the vibrations of ancient dances could be felt in my sleeping bag. I wondered what my next move should be. The fears of complete darkness coupled with these sounds awakened my imagination and convinced me to vacate my nest and seek shelter in my boat anchored offshore. Taking only my sleeping bag, I settled in the boat for the safety of removal from this sacred place. Immediately, as soon as this was accomplished, all activity ceased.

When daylight arrived, I now felt safe in returning to the island to retrieve the supplies left the night before. The campsite was calm, noises of the dawn were as expected and peace and respect encompassed me. I continued my journey north away from Strawberry Island. From then on, my explorations during the remainder of my trip would only be from the safety and security of the boat. Other islands and wilderness terra firma would be viewed only and not violated by my physical presence.

It was after my journey was ended; I visited the Lac du Flambeau Museum and learned of the history and stories surrounding the island. All that was learned, I had experienced. The tales were true, these grounds were sacred and the spirits of ancient times were alive. Thanks to our country's Native American heritage and thanks for allowing me to experience it, (firsthand) so to speak.

Strawberry Island, sometimes known as "Bone Island," is the site of the last battle between the Ojibwe and the Sioux in 1745. It is believed that thousands of warriors clashed that day and hundreds lie dead when the skirmish was finished. Although tribal members from both sides perished, the Sioux were defeated and driven from the area. Today it is the Ojibwe that inhabit the area.

In the late 1880s the federal government gave the island to the Whitefeather family, tribal members, under the Dawes Allotment Act. The Act provided for land distribution to individual American Indians who would be responsible farmers. The usual grant was 160 acres to heads of household and 80 acres to each unmarried adult. Land had to be held for 25 years. The recipients would become citizens of the United States subject to federal and state laws. In 1910 the Whitefeathers sold the island for $2,105 to Edwin Mills, a non-Indian from Colorado, because they believed that there was not enough acreage for productive farming. (Edwin's son died, and he raised his grandson, Walter, who eventually inherited the property. Today, Walter's three children own Strawberry Island.)

In 1967 archeological research teams led by Dr. Robert Salzer of Wisconsin's Beloit College excavated ten sites that yielded information of island occupation dating back to 200 BC or earlier. Evidence of a 19th century village was uncovered as well. Salzar declared the island "the most important archaeological site in northern Wisconsin." In 1978 the island was listed on the National Register of Historic Places. (This listing signifies historical importance of a site. It does not offer protection of the cultural resources.)

Although no burial sites were found, it is a widely held view that the islands hold bodies of inhabitants dating back to phases of the Woodland Traditions (beginning about 500 B.C.). Because the island consists of 26 acres, it is conceivable that the gravesites were not uncovered.

Tribal elders tell of dark nights when they watched the spirits of the island dance around a fire on the island. Others say they heard war cries and screams that they believe is a spiritual re-enactment of the last battle there between the Sioux and the Ojibwe.

There is another story too, of a French missionary who tried to put up a cross to honor the island as a sacred placed. A black bear attacked and killed him, so his ghost allegedly inhabits the island as well.

And yet another story: During the gangster era whiskey was smuggled into the area from Canada. When an informant ratted on the importers, they took him to the island, and he never came back. Another spirit resides on Strawberry Island!

Children are told to stay off the island, not only out of respect, but because the malevolent Sioux spirits may cause harm to future generations of the Ojibwe.

In 1985 Wisconsin passed a new state law (Wisconsin Act 316) incurring penalties for persons who desecrate or vandalize burial sites other than cemeteries (which were already protected). But, again, burial sites are merely *believed* to exist on Strawberry Island.

In 1995 the Mills family applied for a permit to build a retirement home on one of the subdivided lots planned for the island. Their permit was denied; an appeal was upheld.

The Tribe sought to purchase the island back in 1997 at an agreed-upon price of $1.5 million. The Mills family accepted the offer, but it was contingent upon approval of a referendum presented to members of the Tribe. The referendum, held in August 1999, failed. The parties went back to the bargaining table. In 2001 the tribe presented an offer for $800,000. That offer was rejected. In February 2003 a court of appeals upheld the denial of a building permit for the island.

The Mills family claims the last offer they got from the tribe was only $250,000. So in 2008 both sides worked out an agreement. A lease was signed giving a tribal member control of the island. Terms of the lease were not disclosed, but it is known that he would have to approve any sale of the property. It has been stated that the Mills family hoped to assist the tribe in finding a non-profit organization that might develop the island as a reserve, retreat or educational center.

Clouds of mystery hover over Strawberry Island

Sound carries well over water. On a given mid-summer night one might assume there is a powwow at the Indian Bowl with native dancing and drums. Further investigation proves there is no performance that night. The sounds, muffled and eerie, seem to emanate from off the shores of the island. It is July, and spirits of the Sioux, Ojibwe, the French priest and the mob informant are celebrating Miskomini-Giizis—the Raspberry Moon—on Strawberry Island! Listen in wonder, remember the plunder, but stay asunder—let the spirits rest in peace (or not!) on the isle full of history and mystery!

CHAPTER 7

EDGAR OF NORWOOD

I am almost afraid, though I know the night
Lets no ghosts walk in the warm lamplight.
Yet ghosts there are; and they blow, they blow.
Out in the wind and the scattering snow.[7]

Norwood Pines is an elegantly rustic supper club located at the end of a long drive lined with stately pines. A short drive on Highway 70 heading west of Minocqua, Wisconsin, takes you from hustle and bustle to tranquility in less than five minutes.

Snuggled in the midst of a grove of large red pines and warmed by a blanket of fresh sparkling snow, the stately building invites patrons to come inside and warm up in front of a roaring fire.

In warmer weather patrons may partake in the screened-in porch while watching white-tail deer meander into the meadow. Pretty Patricia Lake offers a picture-perfect backdrop.

The Erv Teichmiller family has owned and operated Norwood Pines since 1995. Today sons John and Tom manage the successful business.

A curse was put on the building in the mid 1930s, but it appears that hex has been lifted! And the

---

[7] "Ghosts," Fannie Sterns Davis.

eternal resident of Norwood Pines, *Edgar*, seems to ensure that things continue to run smoothly!

Norwood Pines Supper Club

Norwood Pines was constructed in the late 1930s on a parcel of 200 acres. The 15-room lodge was built by Frank Tillman. There were nine cottages: five fishing cottages and four American-Plan (meals included). It was designed by the same architect who did Little Bohemia (where the Dillinger gang had the famous shootout with the feds). In fact, many gangsters of that era frequented Norwood Pines as well.

Tillman's first wife died in childbirth. His second marriage, to a woman named Martha—who some say was a witch—ended three years after the resort was built. Martha supposedly had an affair with a man she met at Belle Isle, a downtown Minocqua bar and restaurant.

Frank Tilman found himself in bad financial straits. Martha wanted the building; Frank did not want her to have it. He filed for bankruptcy, and Norwood Pines was sold. Martha, however, confiscated furniture from the dining room and placed a curse on the building for future owners.

The next owner was a man named Jacob Huber. According to Erv Teichmiller, Huber's father and sister were subsequently killed in a car accident. Huber later married a woman from Saudi Arabia. Their daughter was kidnapped and never found. A victim of Martha's curse, Huber finally sold the business. At some point, Tillman returned to the area with a newfound wealth. He paid back his debtors and made good with Huber, who had purchased the business not knowing that Martha had absconded with the furniture.

A third owner supposedly died too. So did the man they called Edgar.

Edgar resided in a room above the restaurant. John Teichmiller believes that Edgar managed, not owned, the supper club because his name has not been found on prior deeds. Regardless of whether he hanged himself in that room over a bad relationship with a call girl or a waitress, or whether his life ended when a shady deal with the mob went bad, Edgar has not left the building!

I asked John if there had been any Edgar incidents recently. "Just last Saturday," he began, "a salesman, Daniel, dropped off some product here." John continued to say that his brother, Tom, was on the main floor. Daniel visited the restroom on that floor before leaving. When he came out, he heard Tom talking upstairs. Daniel "hollered goodbye to Tom...and thought it was rude that he didn't answer." Daniel left, and John looked out the window. Tom's truck was gone; he hadn't been in the building at the time!

John regressed to another incident. "About a year and a half ago...we had two tables pushed together for a family that was dining here. There was this little kid. He kept smiling and waving to someone over by the fireplace." The "grandpa" he saw was invisible to anyone else.

"Grandpa has left the building!"

Then there was the time that the building lost power for a period of time. Candles at the tables provided enough light, and ambiance, for the customers who were finishing their dinners. Later, when the only people left in the building were employees, it was noticed that all the candles had been blown out in the back dining room. None of the waitresses had extinguished them. It must have been Edgar!

There was yet another occurrence in the back dining area: That area had been closed, the doors shut. A customer in the front dining area told the bus boy that he saw a man with a trench coat walking in the back room. A waitress went to check it out. Before she could open the door, it "popped open—right in front of her!" There was nobody in the room; the guest in the trench coat was never found.

John Teichmiller shows us the back dining area.

Tom Teichmiller and his wife, Shannon, lived upstairs at Norwood Pines before they moved into their new house. John, working in the dining area the night before they moved, heard them talking upstairs. He went up to join them, but nobody was there. From the upstairs windows John looked out the back of the building; there were no headlights. He looked out front; there were no taillights.

83

Obviously, Tom and Shannon had not been here. John reminisced, "Yet I heard the conversation as clear as day."

Then there were those upper-story windows that wouldn't stay shut! A manager from a local bank was involved with an inspection of the supper club. John recalled walking the manager and his loan officer through the building. Windows that had been closed would now be open. This happened again...and again! Finally, the windows were nailed shut. But the bank manager refused to enter the place again!

The owner previous to the Teichmillers had been in business for 13 years—more than any owner before that. Now the Teichmillers have been here over 13 years. John feels the bad luck curse has been lifted.

It would certainly seem that way. Edgar is still around, but he seems like a benevolent ghost. He helps the waitresses blow out the candles and move the silverware and water glasses around. He likes little kids, and keeps pretty much to himself—even talking to himself. Certainly, one cannot fault Edgar for not wanting to leave the attractiveness and the comforts of the building he has called home for so many years.

CHAPTER 8

STILL SHOTS

Well, the "G" men, "T" men, revenuers, too
Searchin' for the place where he made his brew
They were looking, trying to book him,
But my pappy kept a-cookin'
Whshhooh... white lightnin'[8]

"She was just a moonshiner's daughter, but he loved her still!"

During the Prohibition era, many men found that they could earn better money than the average wage and have a few drinks while they were doing it. Small stills and larger distilleries dotted the Northwoods landscape. Sometimes women were involved too, running the bootlegged liquor to Chicago and other cities.

Charlie Spencer of Boulder Junction, Wisconsin, tells a story about his father who came to northern Wisconsin in the 1920s from Kentucky. He got off at the Winegar (now Presque Isle) train station where he was met by his cousin, bootlegger Melvin Spencer.

The forests near Winegar were filled with virgin timber, dotted with sparkling lakes. This beautiful untamed area was a perfect place to operate their

---

[8] George Jones. "White Lightning."

illicit business, concealed from those who would attempt to arrest them and shut their stills down. These men often trapped beaver, selling the pelts for $25 apiece, an excellent price at the time. Supplement that with income from the illegal production and sale of alcoholic beverages, and one could make a fine living. But the trade could be dangerous, and everyone packed guns!

Most of the extended Spencer family already had or would settle near the Crandon (Wisconsin) area. Full-blown distilleries were set up near Crandon in old barns. Charlie's uncle ran a speakeasy in the basement of an existing downtown Crandon building.

But Dad Spencer was more of a loner. He became involved in a smaller scale moonshine operation. There were many small stills in the area that produced about 7-1/2 gallons each. The illegal liquid was sold in 12-ounce beer bottles for $1 each. (This was the equivalent of a day's wages at that time.) Some of these bottles were transported over to Hurley. But not by the bottle! Much of the moonshine was carried by cask or keg in a back-pack rigging and bottled at the point of sale.

Men moved around in the woods so as not to create a trail that might look suspicious to law enforcement authorities. If the moonshiners suspected intruders, they might tie a rope around their stills and lower them into a boggy area or a lake. It was difficult to detect the small ropes that blended in with the grassy surroundings.

Dad Spencer made high quality whiskey (no hangovers!). It was produced from corn and seasonal fruits and sometimes called *brandy*. It was "high octane liquor", a higher class of booze sold to some resort owners for gangster parties. Winchester was the location of a lot of these gatherings. It was a pretty town with a lot of flowers, neat houses and beautiful lawns. Location was perfect—off the highway far enough to offer sought-after seclusion and secrecy. Well-dressed mob members and their molls would party in big tents with linen tablecloths, drinking the whiskey sold to them by the northern hillbillies.

Charlie's dad was in his mid fifties when Charlie was born. That would put him somewhere in his late twenties when the following event took place. It was years later when Charlie's father told him about the event.

Charlie was working for WXPR radio station and "just happened to have" a recorder along with him to capture the story of the Winegar shootings of August 12, 1926! (Some accounts of the event say August 14.) I listened intently to the description of what happened the afternoon that the constable came to serve papers on one of the men living in shacks near Mermaid Lake close to the Michigan border.

George Rutherford, constable and deputy sheriff at Winegar, accompanied by his wife, drove to the area to serve a warrant on William Stanley. Stanley was being charged by a woman back in Kentucky for killing her husband. A few months prior Rutherford arrested Stanley on the charge, but did not have a warrant. He planned to hold Stanley until he got one. Stanley talked his way out of being handcuffed. Rutherford then let Stanley go into a back room to change clothes. Stanley escaped through a window.

The moonshiners lived in shacks "located in a remote area a fair distance away" from the stills. With Stanley that day was C. L. Boring. According to Spencer, "Boering had told Rutherford more than once to back off; and if he came looking to bust his moonshine operation, he would kill him! He was also being served for not paying child support. He tried to prove he had "paid by buying his ex wife a side of beef." Boering did not know about the warrant being served on Stanley that day.

While his wife sat in the car, Rutherford walked through the woods to the shack where the defendant lived. According to Charlie's dad, "They had run the batch and sampled the wares and were passed out sleeping when Rutherford woke them up at gunpoint. Sheriff Rutherford shoots him (Boering) as the guy brought up his pistol." Reportedly, Boering was hit in his shooting hand. He immediately switched hands and pulled the trigger, hitting Rutherford between the eyes.

Mrs. Rutherford heard two shots very close together. She waited for nearly a half hour. Then, fearful because her husband had not returned to the car, she hurried into Winegar to report the incident. Although nobody was deputized, a posse was formed and quickly headed for the woods. They found Rutherford's body near a still where he had been shot and killed. Sheriff's deputies soon arrived and arrested Boering for the murder. Boering was taken in to Winegar, but scuttled to Eagle River (approximately 50 miles away) when a lynch mob threatened to take over.

That night, a new posse, led by Elmer Monk and a woodsman called *Big Alex* Garis went to look for

William Stanley and another moonshiner, Jerry Brandenberg.

Chet Dumask of Presque Isle remembers the large Russian they called Big Alex. He once said to the then five-year-old Dumask, "I bet that I can pick you up with both hands behind my back." A seemingly impossible task, Dumask thought. Big Alex put his hands behind his back, tightened his teeth on the belt, and lifted young Chet right off the ground!

Dumask also remembers hearing about the shootout following the killing of Constable Rutherford. He says that Brandenberg and Stanley were spotted walking on a road down by Birch Lake (near where Spencer's dad had a speakeasy). According to Dumask, Big Alex and Monk were dropped off at the nearby school and laid in wait for the two.

As Brandenberg and Stanley approached the two men, Monk centered them in the light of his flashlight and hollered, "Halt." Both of the men returned his order with gunfire. The second shot, fired by Stanley, hit Monk in the head and killed him. But not before Monk had a chance to pull the trigger on his double barrel shotgun. Big Alex also fired, and Stanley suffered a fatal wound. Brandenberg escaped in the woods, but was later arrested by yet another posse.

Charlie's dad's first wife was Mattie, Jerry Brandenberg's daughter. Charlie recalls an incident that happened after the Winegar shootout:

> She cheated on my dad, and one day he came home to find her in bed with another man.

The man ran out the bedroom window naked, and my dad shot at him with his 30-30 deer rifle. I asked my dad how he missed. For many years he would not answer the question. Then, finally in his 80s, he admitted that he was 'just trying to scare him.' Knowing my dad's ability to shoot and hit a moving target, I believe his words.

Dad used to set up roofing nails on a board and drive tacks at 30 yards. He rarely missed. He used iron sights, and I still have the .22 rifle that I watched him do it with.

After we talked, Charlie subscribed to an internet service and found scores of articles from all over the country regarding the shootout. According to Charlie, "a lot of them contained false information," but the shootout in the remote area just a few miles from the Michigan border got big-time coverage!

While talking about the killings on that night in August of '26, Charlie digressed to a more general scenario in the area, as big-time criminals, the likes of Capone and Dillinger, came north seeking safe havens when things got hot in the Chicago area.

He asked if I wanted to see where "front men" stayed when they arrived in the Northwoods to make sure "the coast was clear" for their infamous bosses to arrive at the larger resorts such as Little Bohemia.

"Of course," I excitedly replied. Within five minutes from his house, we entered the woods just off Highway 51. Crews were just beginning to log the area, but dilapidated remains of the shacks were still visible. The rental cabins, often used by hunters as well, stood adjacent to the old highway.

Hunting cabins rented by mob henchmen still stand near Old Highway 51 north of Minocqua

Recent shovel marks could be seen; evidence that yet another believer was looking for buried riches left behind by the Dillinger gang.

"I'll show you something else," Charlie said as we trudged through the underbrush. Parts of a rusted old automobile were scattered in an area near the cabins. "Look at this." Charlie picked up the driver's-side car door and showed me a bullet hole. We discussed the possibility that a hunter in bygone years may have used the door for target practice, but it was interesting and exciting to imagine that maybe that hole could have been a result of a gunfight as the driver tried to escape from the authorities.

I borrowed the old door and have used it as a "show-and-tell" item at a book signing and story-telling event, promising Charlie that I would not list it on E-Bay, but return it to the area when I was finished with it. Maybe others will stumble on to it and let their imagination take wing with the whispering wind as they relive one of the many stories and rumors that remain an active piece of the area's past.

Charlie Spencer points to a bullet hole in
an old car door found near the cabins

CHAPTER 9

ROAMER'S ROOST

**Greyish glowing form
Floating across the dark room
Blink and she is gone.**[9]

Frances Whitfield is a petite, but strong and very capable, woman who will tackle almost anything. She, along with her daughter's help, built her own house (that she recently converted into an Art Center). Guys (or at least one particular man) approach her with a line like "I want to meet the woman who owns four chainsaws!" So it was somewhat of a surprise to find that anything could cause this fearless woman to "freak out" and flee from a floating apparition!

Frances is a property manager for Roamer's Resort, located on Little Martha Lake near Mercer, Wisconsin, but more on that in a little bit....

Ruth Leverson of Mercer recalls that her family (the Roamers) purchased the resort in 1946. Her father owned Badger Bearing in Milwaukee, and drove north every weekend. Ruth, her mom, and older brother and sister lived in the two-bedroom dwelling that her dad remodeled in 1955 into a

---

[9] Enid Cleaves. "Specter Spectator", 2010

"humungous" house. Ruth remembers that it was "a perfect place to be raised and a wonderful, beautiful life for us." Her mom rented out the cottages on the property. "She didn't charge much" and renters returned year after year. It was one big, happy family, where the owners and guests played games and took boat trips to the island "near Capone's place." Ruth and her teenage friends sometimes camped out on the island, sleeping on an old box spring that was left there by other campers.

Ruth remembers being invited into the Ralph Capone household the year she was running for Carnival Queen. It was a fund-raising event; the Capones contributed. (Incidentally, Ruth was crowned as queen!)

Brother Al Capone and his henchmen used to visit Ralph, and liked to do a little fishing. The Roamer kids loved playing with the Capone's dog. Later, they would give Ruth and her siblings a cocker spaniel.

Now, back to my story....

I accompanied Frances as she drove to the resort one Saturday morning to make sure that it was clean and ready for the next vacationers that were to arrive later that day. We entered the tree-canopied drive leading to the resort. I remarked how beautiful that it was. And I thought to myself what a wonderful escape house this must have been in the gangster heydays. The authorities would never know where to begin to look for them in this heavily wooded area.

Frances had explained to me that sometime in the early to mid 1900s owners of the resort were reputed money launderers, probably connected to noted criminal elements that found northern Wisconsin a tranquil and inconspicuous place where most people were sympathetic to their illegal activities. Many, in fact, made a fair wage in their employ.

Frances explained that the present owner had again renovated the main lodge. But the "integrity of the old lodge is intact"...and so it seems is one of the former owners!

A set of stairs from the foyer leads to the main floor entrance. "I have to show you something," Frances remarked, and lifted a portion of the stairs up to show me a secret escape from the basement. "On the other end of the basement there is another exit," she added.

Stairs open up to an escape route from the basement.

As it was empty, we were free to wander through the large house. As we did, Frances pointed out all the cubby holes and hidden passages.

The living room has a very large bay window that overlooks the lake. Behind a curio cabinet, there is a small nook, cleverly hidden from view. "This was a good place to monitor the lake," Francis explained. I thought it might be an ingenious place to disappear if there was a knock on the door. The visitor could peer into an empty living room while the maid explained that the owner was not at lodge that day.

Back of curio cabinet opens to hidden cubby hole

There was another disguised door that led to the maid's closet upstairs. From there, one could pull off a wall panel and get to the roof.

Ruth Leverson recalled that her mom would "store things" in the hidden cubby hole behind the curio cabinet and that she would keep her pies cool in the tunnel leading up to the bedroom area. Ruth also recalls hiding on a shelf in a "secretive area" just two steps up from the tunnel area.

After touring the home, we lingered for a while in the dining room. "This is where I was when I saw her," Frances remembers. "I was here on a winter evening doing electrical work. My power shut off, so this room and the living room were dark. I had a headlight on my head while I worked. I was very intent, very focused." Then she caught a glimpse of something out of the corner of her eye. "This woman came down from the stairway into the living room and was headed for the stairs to the lower level. She didn't seem to notice that I was there."

Frances was repairing this light fixture
the night she saw the ghost

Frances remembers the woman looked like she was wearing a sweatshirt and jeans and appeared to be "translucent, grayish, gauzy." Though it was dark, the apparition appeared to have a glow as she "floated" through the living room. "I remember thinking at the time that she is going down stairs— and there shouldn't be anyone else in the house!" Frances continued, "I exited the house, left all the lights on, and went home because I was so freaked out..."

Many months after the incident, some people from Alaska came to visit the house. One of them stated that he had worked here when he was sixteen. He had pictures with him. Frances recognized a person in one of the pictures. The lady in the photo was Jean Roamer, the phantom that Frances believes she saw the night she was repairing the dining room light.

Ruth Leverson said that she had not seen a ghost during the period she lived there, but mentioned that her grandmother had passed away in her upstairs bedroom shortly after watching the John F. Kennedy funeral in 1963. Ruth's mother, Jean Roamer, died on September 21, 2008 and is buried in Mercer.

Frances agreed the maybe Jean resembled her mother (Ruth's grandmother). And, the sweatshirt and jeans just might have been a long dress—more compatible with the clothing worn by women of that time.

Frances and I talked about ghosts reappearing during periods of construction or remodeling. "Well, Rob (the current owner) saw her too." He and his partners had done significant remodeling just a few months prior to when I saw her...and, I was installing lights that would change things in the house!"

I conjure up images in my mind of the phantom of the "Roost" peering out of the upstairs bedroom window to see if a float plane had landed with illegal booze from Canada. Then, she floats down the stairs, and through the dining room wall, as she looks for someone to tell the hired men that they need to bring trucks down to the lake to unload the contraband from the plane.

Maybe the ghost is the former owner who died in the bedroom, or maybe she is a guest who visited the resort, or even a lady of the evening or gangster moll. But then, maybe the ghost is from a more recent era. Or maybe there is more than one spirit inhabiting Roamer's Roost.

But, whoever she (or they) was in a past human life, the spirit now doesn't want to leave this beautiful home overlooking picturesque Little Martha Lake. (That seems to be my repetitive answer to why there is a ghost in a building, doesn't it?)

CHAPTER 10

DANCES WITH SNAKES

We are brothers
Born of the earth
And born of the sun
And our destiny is only one another's
However apart the races we have run.[10]

Barbara and John McFarland of Manitowish Waters, Wisconsin are internationally renowned artists working out of their Woodsholm gallery located in their lovely home overlooking the Trout River on the Manitowish chain of ten lakes. Former owners and operators of a large cranberry operation, they seem content now to travel and create their works of art.

Barbara likes to "search out mythic images which whisper, sing and howl around me." Her paintings center on the life of the Ojibwe and "incorporate the spirit of the ancient indigenous cultures."

John explains that his art "is motivated by my own desire to capture images which have special significance to me, images which evoke a deep spiritual or personal connection with the subject."

---

[10] Witter Bynner. "Snake Dance," circa. 1920.

With, and perhaps because of, their creative, artistic minds, the two share a commonality: sensitivity beyond the physical, natural realm that extends into the spiritual, psychic world.

Things appear and disappear within their Manitowish Waters home regularly, and garage doors open and shut quietly for no apparent reason. Both Barbara and John sometimes see "black wings flying around in their bedroom." They have seen the moving shadows in other houses they have lived in as well!

While some events are just perplexing, others are extremely vexing!

There was the time in Provence, France when John lost his passport. (I'm sure a vision raced through his head of airport security and embassy guards!) The couple scoured their hotel room thoroughly. Concerned, John and Barbara discussed what they were going to do. Then they both turned around; "the passport was right in the middle of the bed." There was no logical explanation.

Then there was the Horrible Hotel in the "Windy City." On the way back to northern Wisconsin from a relative's funeral in southern Indiana, John, Barbara and her parents decided to spend the night in downtown Chicago. The parents settled into a bright, cheery room. John opened the door to their room just down the hall and brought in their luggage. As Barbara went into the bathroom, John sat down on the bed. John described their room as "dark and unappealing." He suddenly felt overwhelmed with sadness. Barbara, on the other hand, experienced a somewhat different emotion: horror! She had the "vision of blood everywhere in the bathroom." Unaware of what his wife was experiencing, John's immediate thought was: "We've got to get out of this room." He remembers thinking that "whatever this is, it has the need to go—and it wants to come with us."

Hurriedly they grabbed their luggage and walked over to the parents' room. "We can't stay here!" They all left and went to spend the night with friends in the city.

And there was that evening in beautiful Barcelona, Spain. The city was lovely, with lots of fun, artistic things to see and do. After a wonderful dinner, the couple walked along the water. The Black Hats (security squad) were out in force, keeping the outdoors safe for tourists such as John and Barbara. The two wandered into a small courtyard. They stopped somewhere in the middle of it when John got this "horrible image of people screaming, machine guns being fired—a tremendous bloodletting was going on...perhaps an execution or a revolution." In March 1938 Italian aircraft bombed Barcelona, killing over 1,000 and injuring thousands more. The Germans used Spain to test their new military equipment, and the Spanish Civil War occurred in the late 1930s, costing millions of lives. But here, in the courtyard, John found himself in the middle of whatever battle or event was taking place at that instance!

But the story that relates to Wisconsin's Northwoods is not that of a political revolution, a hotel execution, or even a gangster, but a visit from an American Indian snake dancer!

It all began when Barbara was asked to do a painting for an auction at a fund raiser for the local (Minocqua) Howard Young Medical Center.

Barbara had read an article in the Rotogravure Section of the *Chicago Tribune* about an artist named Edward Curtis. One of his photographs was that of a Hopi Snake Dancer.

The dancers hold bull snakes, as well as the poisonous whip snakes and rattlesnakes, in their mouths and hands while stroking them gently with an eagle feather so they will not bite. After the lengthy dance, the snakes are returned to the desert. Here, they are to relay the Hopi prayers for rain to the Gods underneath the ground. With an affinity for American Indian art, Barbara set out to paint a likeness of the Curtis photograph.

Barbara recalls that it was the night before the fund raiser and she was running a bit behind on her work. So it was sometime "in the wee hours of the morning when the painting was completed." For no apparent reason, a strange and sorrowful feeling came over Barbara, and she "started crying for no reason."

The next morning she hurriedly dropped off her finished painting at the sale and drove back from Minocqua. Within a short time Barbara noticed that the newspaper article had disappeared. Also, she had not taken the time to make her usual journal entry with details of her painting. All Barbara remembers was that a local lady, perhaps in her 70s, had purchased her painting—its name seems to be gone forever too.

The couple recalled the events of the September night that the snake dancer made a visit to their home.

John began. "I woke up about 3 a.m., aware that someone was standing next to me on my (left) side of the bed." He "had a feeling that this person was the one from Barbara's painting." He further recalls that "no words were spoken." John "sensed that he wanted me to go with him."

"I can't go, unless you can tell me for sure that I can come back." He could not leave Barbara and did not feel that he could determine whether the person "was real or not."

Next, there was a "loud bang, like a door slamming, and their dog started to bark." John drifted back to sleep.

When he awoke in the morning, John rationalized that "this was a dream," and was relating the experience to his wife. Looking a bit perplexed, Barbara recalled waking to see John standing next to the bed on the side where he always slept. She described the figure as a bit "foggy," like she wasn't completely awake.

"That wasn't me; I couldn't get out of bed." John explained. It seems that the related visions happened at the same time, because Barbara heard the loud noise and the dog bark too.

After doing some research on the snake dancer, Barbara realized that she had finished the painting on the date of the autumn equinox. Today, Hopi tribes continue to celebrate their annual ceremonial snake dance at this time!

John and Barbara McFarland pose with the Edward Curtis photograph that led to the appearance of the snake dancer

Now, you may say that this family has no ties to gangsters (and this is a book about gangsters *and* ghosts), but there is actually one slight connection: John's grandfather (his mother's father) was killed in a car accident in the late 1920s while driving back to his home in Hayward, Wisconsin. Dr. Trowbridge had treated bullet wounds incurred by some gangsters. Though officially called a single-car accident (the car turned over upon Trowbridge), many, including the family, felt that he was actually killed by other members of the mob who sought to protect the identity of the wounded men that the doctor had aided.

CHAPTER 11

SIMPLY SPECTERS

We never saw the ghost, though he was there—
We knew from the raindrops tapping on the eaves.
We never saw him, and we didn't care.

Each day, new sunshine tumbled through the air;
Evenings, the moonlight rustled in dark leaves.
We never saw the ghost, though: he was there.

If ever, when the wind tousled our hair
And prickled goose bumps up and down thin sleeves;
We never saw him. And we didn't care...

To step outside our room at night, or dare
Click off the nightlight; call it fear of thieves
We never saw the ghost; though he was there.

In sunlit dust motes drifting anywhere,
In light-and-shadow, such as the moon weaves.
We never saw him, though, and didn't care.

Until at last we saw him everywhere.
We told nobody. Everyone believes
We never saw the ghost (if he was there),
We never saw him and we didn't care.[11]

This chapter is not about gangsters, but about local people who have been eager to tell me their stories about ghostly experiences of their own.

---

[11] "Ghost Villanelle," Dan Lechay.

A neighbor at the end of our street, ten-year old Olivia McFarland, never saw the ghost—but she knew it was there!

"I was trying to fall asleep one night. Dad and Frances were reading—I always like them to be up when I fall asleep." Olivia was in her bottom bunk bed in a small room that has since been converted into a dining room.

Olivia stands near the window where she saw a light.

She continued, "I saw a bright flash through the window" in the back of the house facing the woods. She was not afraid because she was not alone, so went to the window and peered out. "I saw a flashlight with a light, but there was no body!" There was no car, no person, just the bright light shining from a flashlight suspended in air about five feet from her bedroom window! Olivia thought that if she got out of bed, the ghost might follow her.

Now Olivia was wide awake! "Oh my gosh; when am I going to be able to fall asleep?" She never saw the ghost, but he was there!

Olivia believes in ghosts and that they are benevolent. She doesn't think there are bad ghosts—just some that "might want to tease" her. Perhaps this one was doing just that. It happened just days after her tenth birthday—on April Fool's Day!

****

Olivia's dad, Brent McFarland, has seen a ghost in this house too--many times. So has Frances Whitfield, Brent's fiancée. Not the ghost with no body, but a fully clothed apparition that frequently visits the same home! Frances described the phantom that lives with them.

"There is a slender woman who walks through the house from the entrance hallway through the kitchen, through the dining room, and then disappears." She always follows this west-to-east path through the house." Frances continued. "She is a grey figure wearing a (grey) cloak or blanket wrapped around her...she seems very intent on going somewhere...with a purpose."

Brent added, "She is moving, almost like someone walking down the street. She is not aware of us." Brent believes the figure has longer dark hair,

109

pulled back, and is a bit elusive. He describes that he sees her in his peripheral vision.

Brent and Frances dressed in their
phantom's favorite color: grey

The house they live in is the old McFarland homestead, moved in the late 1980s from the spot where it was built on the cranberry marsh across the river, to its present location. To Brent's knowledge, nobody died in that house.

Brent provides an interesting theory though. Their home is located near Nelson Lake, believed to be a camping site for Ojibwe Indian tribes many decades ago. Perhaps the spirit comes from the land.

The land is close to Wild Rice Lake, too. Supposedly, that lake came to be only when the dam was erected and the Manitowish Waters' chain of ten lakes was formed. Yet, the Trout River flowed through the area then, and it still fills the lakes and channels of the chain. (The Manitowish River does

the same from a different direction; both flow over
the dam in downtown Manitowish Waters.)

Frances speculates that the spirit is from a tribe
that gathered wild rice from the beds in the area.
Maybe there was a settlement here, or perhaps it
was just a good place for the Ojibwe to erect a
campsite during harvesting season.

Brent's daughter stays with the couple every other
week. Olivia has a "battery-operated doorbell" in
her bedroom. Sometimes it goes off when nobody is
in the room. Brent feels that somehow the activities
of the ghost and the doorbell are related.

I asked Brent how often the grey lady appears.
"She may be inactive for sometimes three to four
months." Frances added that she passes through
an average of maybe once a month. "She was just
here; maybe a couple of weeks ago."

****

Mary Rybak lives on the old family farm on Slim
Lake near Butternut, Wisconsin. She saw the
ghost, and recognized her as well!

Mary Rybak relates her story.

Mary's grandmother died of cancer when she was in her early 70s. Grandmother "would have these visions about horses that got away from the owner and be running along with the carriage," Mary remembers, "and then someone would pass on after these premonitions."

Mary doesn't think that she inherited any psychic capabilities, but she knows what she saw! It happened about 15 years ago. She awoke from a deep sleep and opened her eyes. At the foot of her bed was this figure: "a chubby lady with dark brown hair, wearing a dark shirtwaist dress with buttons down the front." The apparition did not speak to her, but Mary had seen pictures, so knew that the apparition was a younger version of her grandmother!

Mary admitted that she did not know there was reported to be a connection between ghostly activity and remodeling of a residence. But she mentioned that they had been "fixing up the house, doing quite a bit of remodeling." So she asked the question: "Are you okay with this, grandma? It was like grandmother was saying that everything was fine!"

****

Joe Mudgett lives in the same 1918 home where he grew up. His mother died of cancer fifteen years ago. She was in hospice, but died suddenly. "None of us were there when she died," Joe laments. "But we'll always remember the time." On that morning Joe remembers waking up to see his mother standing at the foot of the bed. It was 4:46 a.m. She smiled at Joe as if to say "things are just fine." Then she left. Joe's sister, some twenty miles away, saw her in her bedroom too...exactly at 4:46 a.m.

Mom returns to visit...several times a year. She was born on December 27. The family usually sees her a day or two before or after that date each year. The whole family sees her: Joe's 26-year-old daughter, his two sons (age 22 and 32 respectively), and the dog! She appears to all family members—but not to Joe's wife!

Mom smoked, but didn't want Dad to know. So she would sneak outside, have a cigarette, and returned to the house. Joe sees the doorknobs turn, and doors open by themselves. She just never could give up that bad habit!

Mom had always wanted a full porch—a wrap-around deck with a patio. She never got to see it—at least while she was alive! Joe finished the project in October 2006. A week later, and then again several weeks later, Joe saw her walking around on the deck—giving her approval I suspect!

Joe's mom visits him frequently

Joe related another story:

Things will get changed around in the living room, We'll find three or four Hummel

113

figurines moved from the fireplace mantel to the top of the TV. Mom had always wanted a TV like this. It was like she was telling me 'I see that.'

We'll be watching TV. The dog looks anxiously at the patio door, going slightly crazy. I feel a cold breeze; then I see the figure of a body. My grandson saw a reflection in the glass door. And the dog's like, 'What's up, Mom?'

****

Cheri Stratte is a member of a writer's group that meets monthly at the local Your Arts Program. Cheri invited me to contact her mom who had an experience with the supernatural many years ago.

"Mom" relates a story about a time when she was about twelve years old. Her aunt and cousin were visiting from Sheboygan. She and her cousin, Richie, were in the smaller bedroom upstairs looking for a game or some toys to play with. This bedroom, though it had a bed and a dresser in it, served as a junk room with trunks and boxes scattered throughout the room.

In the process of looking for something to occupy their time that day, they watched a nearby box "slide across the floor for about two feet." Excited, they raced down the stairs to tell their mothers.

"You're just playing games with us, you stinkers," was the response the children received—but they knew better! Someone, some thing, had moved the heavy box.

Nothing strange seemed to happen after the incident. Their home was a "warm, comfortable old-fashioned house—with good memories." And, most ghosts are benevolent!

The home has been moved, and converted into the Conservatory of the Arts. It sits across from the movie theatre in Woodruff and next to Dr Kate museum.

The balcony (upper right in picture) is
just off the former "junk room."

****

Parents of a friend of mine, we will call them Carol and Carl, recall happenings in the house they owned in the Minocqua area. Their daughter lives there now; she claims *Henry* is still residing in the home.

Years ago, Carol's dad lived with them. While the kids were in school and he was at the house alone, he would hear music coming from upstairs. He would yell "Turn the noise down," thinking his grandkids were home from school. Soon, everything would be quiet, and a bit later the kids would come home from school! In fact, when Henry thought the noise was too loud, he would inform everyone of his dissatisfaction by flicking the lights on and off.

Footsteps would be heard after everyone was in bed, the family dog would bark at something in the house not seen by human occupants, and a knocking noise seemed to emanate from the attic. Macramé planters inside the home would start to sway, and vases and knick knacks would tip over for no conceivable reason! A grey figure was seen "coming out of one wall and walking through another." Cold spots, and even a white mist, would pass through a room.

Carl recalls getting out of bed and getting dressed one winter evening to investigate a tapping noise outside their bedroom. The minute he stepped out of the house, the noise stopped—and never started again!

Another time, expecting his grandson's arrival, Carl heard the kitchen door open. You guessed it: nobody was there!

A ladder, normally stored in the garage, would be standing against a window. It was winter; there were no tracks in the snow and no clues as to how or why the ladder would be there. (Could it be that Henry was locked out and wanted to come in where it was warm?)

At times the family felt they were being watched. They would catch glimpses of a "face in a window, look again, and it was gone."

After grandpa had passed on, the youngest daughter, eight years old at the time, was playing in the yard with a friend. "Who is that man standing there?" the friend asked her playmate. "Oh, that's my grandpa," was the reply.

One night the same daughter saw her grandfather again, dressed in a white suit and standing at the foot of her bed. He seemed to be assuring her that "everything will be OK."

Years later, the youngest daughter, along with her three-year-old child, visited her sister. After putting the little girl to bed, the sisters chatted. Suddenly the child screamed; the lights and TV went off and the ceiling fan started up on its own and began to rotate "really fast."

A former owner died in the house. His name is not known, but it could be Henry. Regardless, the family believes that he is not an evil spirit and states that "nothing bad happened."

Reminiscing, Carl laments the spirit "just lived there...never cleaned the house, never did the dishes." Seems that he was too busy doing other things!

****

A good friend of mine lost her mother recently. She had been in the nursing home; if and when she was able, she would be transferred to an assisted living home. But, along with the weather, her mom took a turn for the worse. The family was gathered around

117

her bedside. The window, not far from the bed, was open. "You better shut the window and move away from it," the nurse warned as storm clouds darkened and the wind picked up. "We must leave the window open," replied one of the daughters." She then expounded on the old legend that says a departed spirit leaves through an open window. As the family looked out the window, it was obvious that bad storms were passing over their homestead, just a few miles away. The wind died; it was surely the calm before the storm. It was then that she took her last breath. A gust of wind suddenly blew the curtain inwardly; then just as quickly, sucked the curtains back against the stream. Mom's soul had left the building.

****

My husband passed away in December 2010, just two weeks after being diagnosed with pancreatic cancer. He actually died at the home of our good friend, Roxanne. We had made the difficult three-hour trip down to Oshkosh (in central Wisconsin) for a bon voyage party where Bob rallied to say his goodbyes to several friends from the area where we spent most of our adult lives. Many who visited that day were from the Green Apple Folk Society, an organization that Bob had been associated with for years and had sang and entertained both as a solo performer and as a member of the "Crystal River Trio" with his close friends, Gary and Pete. He even sang a song with them at his party; and we all were in tears when Gary sang a song that he had written for Bob about what their friendship meant to him.
Just three days later, the morning after his family gathered around him, Bob left us—unable to make the trip back to the Northwoods that we had called home for the last fourteen years.

I called a friend, Pat Griedl, on the morning of December 22, the day after Bob died. About a month later, I sat with Pat and her husband, Dan, at a friend's wedding reception. In the course of conversation, Dan looked at me and asked, "Have I talked to you since Bob died?" I responded in the negative. Dan proceeded to tell me a story.

Dan has maintained an apartment in a 100-year-old hotel in Fennimore, Wisconsin (in the southwestern part of Wisconsin) for over seven years—since his company transferred him to that area. He commutes on weekends to the home he and Pat share in Appleton.

Dan prefaced his story with the fact that he had not heard any stories of ghosts inhabiting the hotel, nor had anything strange happened while he was living in the building—until about six months before Bob's passing.

Just about every evening Dan started noticing movement out of the corner of his eyes (sometimes on the left side, other times out of his right eye). The movement was always in his peripheral vision; if he looked directly at the source of movement, he would see nothing. Dan perceived the motion to be about three feet off the floor and described it much like a "dog would move" (at that level). It became a normal activity that Dan feels was not related in any way to a vision problem.

Dan recalls that on December 21 "the activity was much greater." He described the movement in his peripheral vision as "higher now, and more intense...definitely something different today." He remembers thinking "that Bob had probably passed away" and that his energy was now passing through his apartment. "I talked to him briefly," Dan recalls. "I said that I hoped that he was in peace. I said that we can choose our friends and that we chose you. Tears were in my eyes." Then the movement decreased, and finally it went away. And Dan has seen nothing since.

Dan Griedl

I found it interesting that the six-month period Dan speaks of coincides with the time frame that we knew Bob was sick—although his disease was not yet diagnosed. Dan agrees; in fact, he feels that the "energies were doing something to get ready" for Bob's final day on earth. With a belief that energy from a death manifests itself in various ways, Dan feels strongly that Bob's energy definitely was with him on the 21st.

I asked Dan if he had any other psychic experiences. He replied, "When my mother passed away." His mom experienced a heart attack in December of 1990, but was doing fine. Dan and Pat were camping in Door County (Wisconsin's "thumb") in July 1991. As they were getting ready to pack up their gear, Dan had a strong feeling that "we needed to get home *now*." At home there was a phone message saying that they should come to the hospital—where they found that his mom was on life support. She died shortly thereafter.

Roxanne related another incident that happened a few weeks after Bob's death. She noticed a strong smell of cinnamon in the room where he died. At first she thought her dog, Nara (or as Bob called her: "Destructo-dog"), had gotten into something in the kitchen and dragged it into the room. After a thorough sensory search of the room, no origin of the odor could be found. She went to the living room, where Nara sometimes deposits her new-found tasty treats; nothing there. Bob loved cinnamon. "I think Bob was trying to communicate with me," Roxanne related.

OK...I'm waiting for a sign from Bob. His ashes *are* under *my* bed (waiting to be distributed over his favorite area). "When are you going to send a message to *me*?" I addressed the box under the bed.

Several nights later I turned out the lights and headed for the stairway to my upstairs bedroom. The moment I stepped on the landing, I heard a strange noise—I can't even describe it. It was sort of like a raspy rustling sound. Only a couple of seconds, and then it was gone. A friend was in bed on the main floor, and another was in her bedroom in the lower level of the house. I'm sure it wasn't from either of them...maybe I was hearing things!

I had heard rustling noises before—twice on the same night—but at a friend's house. It was coming from somewhere at the foot of my bed in the guest room. Or was I dreaming?

121

About a week after the raspy noise caused me to stop and wonder, I was preparing a breakfast casserole—one of those that you assemble the night before and refrigerate until morning. I filled the blender, placed it on its base, plugged it in and started it...well, tried. Nothing happened. I tried two other outlets without any success. After a breakfast the next morning of a poorly blended and baked soufflé, I debated tossing the blender into the garbage bag. For whatever reason, I decided to try it again in the outlet that I started with the previous evening. It whirred and purred like a kitten! The thought occurred to me that this was one of Bob's favorite breakfasts, and he may have been unhappy because he could not join us!

There is a citrus plant in my living room, given to me many years ago by Dan and Pat Griedl. I replanted it once in a larger, but slimmer planter. In its new home the plant grew like a beanstalk toward the ceiling. I replanted it later in a larger pot, and it continued to grow. When it reached the ceiling, I anchored it. It continues to grow across the top of the fireplace. As I remember back to two or three days after Bob died, I noticed a couple of new sprouts growing from the stalk. And I recall thinking, "I wonder when those started growing?" Quite likely, just a coincidence...but it had been months since new growth had appeared.

We scattered Bob's ashes on Memorial weekend. On the way home, we stopped at a Lake Superior beach to look for pretty stones. Layna, Bob's oldest daughter, scraped away the top layer of rocks and sand. A stone, about the size of a quarter, stood out from all the rest. It was a beautiful white and red striated agate that she took to a rock shop to polish. She plans to make the gem into a piece of jewelry—a gift from her father on the day his ashes flew with the eagles!

And, yet, another story about Bob, as told by his youngest daughter, Amber:

When I was a child, my dad would sing *Puff the Magic Dragon* to me almost every night. I thought I would carry on that tradition after my daughter was born, but I could never remember the words. After about my third attempt I gave up. Hayden was two and a half when Daddy passed away. A few months after his death, she suddenly started singing the chorus, every word perfectly clear. I convinced myself that she had learned it at Mother's Day Out (a daycare center for kids). This went on for several weeks. Finally, one day, when we were in the car with my mother, I asked her, 'Hayden, who taught you that song?' Without hesitation she joyfully said, 'Bumpa!' That is her name for my father. I felt goose bumps rising on my skin and asked her, 'When did Bumpa sing that to you?' She said, 'When I take a nappy.' What saddened me more than anything about my father's passing is that Hayden would never know what a fabulous Bumpa she had. Knowing that he is with her fills my heart with such happiness, it brings tears to my eyes.

Amber and Hayden

In early July Roxanne and her mom, Edye, were visiting me for the weekend. We stayed up late on Friday night, playing a few rousing rounds of Hearts, one of our favorite card games. We were all in bed by midnight.

The next morning Edye recalled that my phone rang. She said that she had looked at her watch; it was 12:15. Roxanne mentioned that she had been reading in her bedroom downstairs. She heard someone talking as in a phone conversation. I was upstairs, probably asleep, and heard nothing. A check of "Caller ID" on my phone showed no calls coming in at that time. A couple of hours later that morning we found out Bob's dad died in Virginia about 7 p.m. the night before. "It must have been Bob" (who had called), Edye said matter-of-factly.

I believe it was in April, about four months after Bob died that the most convincing incident that has ever happened to me...happened! I was relaxing on the deck off the master bedroom. As I got up from the chair to go into the house, I saw this little cloud—maybe about 3 feet long—drift into my line of vision, between the pine trees and my house. As I watched it approach the front side of the deck, it slowly dissipated in front of me! I remember thinking: maybe this is smoke—Bob is having one more cigarette and laughing because I can't do or say anything to him about it!

I had always said that I never received a premonition, got a message from beyond, or seen a ghost. But...maybe I have. The above-mentioned incidents certainly beg the question. And, I once watched a misty form undulate across my hotel room where a former maid, since deceased, purportedly spends time. Or, maybe it was just my eyes adjusting after watching the light on the ceiling blink.

I hear strange noises many times. Sometimes I think that I hear a car approaching or the slam of a car door. I look outside; there is no car—neither in my driveway nor at our neighbor's place.

Last fall I heard a witch-like voice at the screen door: a drawn-out "Hell...Ohh" with a lower intonation of the last syllable. Nobody was there. *What possessed me* to believe there was?!

As far as gangsters go, I probably have seen people who could qualify as such, and the descendents of those who operated outside of the law and frequented their Northwoods hideouts back in the 1920s and 1930s still live in the area.

But ghosts? Where once I could only say that "I wouldn't have a *ghost of a chance*" in recognizing one, I can now hope that I will be aware enough to recognize the phenomenon as it presents itself, rather than explain it away in the fashion that I have been accustomed to!

Like good wine, ghostly activity is something that should improve with age. Think about it; every year, the total number of persons who have departed this life increases. So, more and more spirits may be lingering here on earth. Like a fine musical instrument, though, we must keep our senses well tuned to recognize the signs. (*Get into the spirit,* so to speak!)

Happy Hauntings!

SELECTED BIBLIOGRAPHY

Articles, Books and Newspapers

Capone, Deirdre. *Uncle Al Capone, The Untold Story From Inside His Family.* ReCap Publications, Inc. Bronx, NY, 2010.

Hollatz, Tom. *Gangster Holidays, The Lore and Legends of the Bad Guys.* St. Cloud, MN: North Star Press of St. Cloud, Inc.

Laabs, Joyce. "Norwood Pines: Martha's 'curse' lingers on," *The Lakewood Times,* October 28, 2005.

"Looking Back: Dillinger Returns," *The Lakeland Times,* September 25, 2000.

Mason, Kathy S. "Mystery at Sand Point Lighthouse,"*Michigan History* (Sept./Oct. 2003): 21-27

Mercer Remembers...Pictures & Stories of its Past, Presented by The Mercer Area Historical Society, 1998.

Molzahn Ken. Reproduction article on John Dillinger, *Historical Fish Wrap, 2009.* Green Bay, WI.

"Nominate Strawberry Island for the National Register," *The Lakeland Times,* January 14, 2004 reproduction of original 1978 article.

"Posse Arrests 3 Kentuckians," Ironwood MI *Daily Globe,* August 13, 1926.

Skubal, Michael. "Depp Movie to be Filmed in Northwoods," *Rhinelander Daily News,* February 6, 2008.

Van Goethem, Larry. "Haunted or not, house to be razed," *The Milwaukee Journal,* February 11, 1985.

Vogel, Virgil J. "Indian Names in Michigan."

White, Rachel. "Jeffords bring the Hide-A-Way back to life – 'hauntings' and all," *The Lakeland Times,* March 25, 2011.

Interviews

Brunner, Peg. The Mercer Area Historical Society, Mercer, WI (August 2010)

Dietz, Judy. Summerwind experience (July 2011)

Dumask, Chet. Presque Isle, WI colorful history. August 8, 2011.

Griedl, Dan. Energy in motion. (May 2011).

Hallock, Roxanne. Cinnamon scent. (January 2011).

Leverson, Ruth. Roamer's Roost. (October 23, 2010).

McFarland, Barbara and John. Family psychic experiences, (August 26, 2010).

McFarland, Brent. Ghost in family homestead, (March 2011)

McFarland, Olivia. Flashlight in the window, (August 19, 2010).

Mudgett, Joseph. Ghost in family homestead, (August 24, 2010).

Raychel, Ray. Experiences on Strawberry Island, Lac du Flambeau (July 2009).

Rybak, Mary. Ghost story in family homestead, (August 24, 2010).

Scalf, Jeff. Great nephew of John Dillinger, (July 23, 2011).

Spencer, Charlie. Stories of stills and gangster activities in the northwoods. (March 17, 2010).

Stratte, Cheri and her mom. Story of ghost in the old family homestead, now the Conservatory of Arts in Woodruff, WI.

Teichmiller John and his father, Erv. Edgar, the ghost at Norwood Pines. (February 2010).

Wagner, Jerry. Extra in movie "Public Enemies" (May 2008).

Whitfield, Frances. Experience at Roamer's Resort, Mercer, WI and other encounters (July 2010, March 2011).

Web Sites

"Al Capone, a Notorious Prohibition Era Gangster," www.associatedcontent.com

"Al Capone Biography," www.notablebiographies.com

"Al Capone's Grave," www.hollywoodusa.co.u

"Al Capone's Grave and Ghost Claims," www.geocities.com

"Baby Face Nelson," www.everything2.com

"Baby Face Nelson, Childlike Mug, Psychopathic Soul," Joseph Geringer. www.trutv.com

"Backyard Traveler by Rich Moreno," www.backyardtraveler.blogspot.com

"Biography: Al Capone," www.angelfire.com

"Biography for Al Capone," www.imdb.com

"Calumet, Michigan," www.absoluteastronomy.com

"Capone's Tax Trial and Downfall," www.myalcaponemuseum.com

"Class War at Christmas," John Newsinger. www.socialistreview.org

"Depp Movie to be Filmed in Northwoods," by Michael Skubal. www.rhinelanderdailynews.com Feb. 6, 2008

"Eddie O'Hare and Son," www.snopes.com Feb. 2005

"Eliot Ness," www.en.wikipedia.org

Facebook.com/pages/Strawberry Island

"Federal Bureau of Investigation—FBI History—Famous Cases, www.fbi.gov

"Ghost Stories: Summerwind," www.paranormalstories.blogspot.com

"The Haunting of Al Capone," www.prairieghosts.com

"Italian Hall Disaster," www.en.wikipedia.org

"Jonathan Carver's Footprints: The Carver Land Grant Case of 1825 and the Impact of American Indian Policy." www.minds.wisconsin.edu

"Local Descendent Stakes Claim to Strawberry Island," Doug Etten *The Lakeland Times.* www.lakelandtimes.com 6-13-08.

"Norwood Pines Marks 70 Years of a Long, Rich History," Joyce Laabs, *The Lakeland Times.* www.lakelandtimes.com/main August 8, 2008.

Obituaries, Lewandoski, Jean E. www.host.madison.com/news/local/article

"On the Trail of Al Capone in Allegan County," Charlotte Weick, www.mlive.com

"Reputed Capone Hideout Sold to Wisconsin bank,"
Stephanie Chen, October 8, 2009.
www.cnn.com/2009/CRIME

"The Sioux Warriors of Strawberry Island," Dennis
Boyer. www.w-files.com/files/gh_strawberry island

"Sub Development on Strawberry Island,"
www.studios.com/ojibweuseum

"Summerwind: Wisconsin's Most Haunted House,"
www.prairieghosts.com

"Was Robert P. Lamont Truly Haunted?"
www.home.att.net

Poems, Songs

Anka, Paul and Sinatra, Frank. *My Way*. 1969.

Bryant, William Cullen. *An Indian at the Burial
Place of his Fathers.*

Bynner, Witter. *Snake Dance*. Circa 1925

Capone, Alphonse. *Maddona Mia*. Circa early 1930s

Cleaves, Enid. Specter Spectator. 2010

Davis, Fanny Sterns. *Ghosts*

Frost, Robert. *Ghost House.*

Guthrie, Woody. *Nineteen Thirteen Massacre*. 1941

Lechay, Dan. *Ghost Villanelle*. 2003

Mayer, Henry and Mercer, Johnny. *Summer Wind.*
1965

Service, Robert W. *Bank Robber*

Torrey, Day. *Baby Face Nelson*

Museums and Miscellaneous

ABC News special regarding Al Capone's prison
music, April 17, 2009.

Coppertown Mining Museum, Calumet, MI. July 5,
2009.

The Mercer Area Historical Society, Mercer, WI.
August 2010.

Presque Isle Historical Society, Presque Isle, WI.
August 2011.

Slide Presentation: *Gangsters of the Northwoods,*
Mercer, WI Community Center. Presented to
students of the Mercer Environmental Tourism
Charter School and sponsored by the Mercer
Education Foundation. October 2008.